The Irregular at Magic High School

ESCAPE ARC II

25

Tsutomu Sato

Illustration Kana Ishida

YEN ON
NEW YORK

THE IRREGULAR AT MAGIC HIGH SCHOOL
TSUTOMU SATO

Translation by Kenia A. Hara
Cover art by Kana Ishida

MAHOUKA KOUKOU NO RETTOUSEI Vol. 25 ESCAPE HEN (GE)

Edited by Dengeki Bunko
First published in Japan in 2018 by KADOKAWA CORPORATION, Tokyo.
English translation rights arranged with KADOKAWA CORPORATION, Tokyo, through Tuttle-Mori Agency, Inc., Tokyo.

Yen On
150 West 30th Street, 6th Floor
New York, NY 10001

Visit us at yenpress.com
facebook.com/yenpress
twitter.com/yenpress
yenpress.tumblr.com
instagram.com/yenpress

First Yen On Edition: May 2025
Edited by Yen On Editorial: Rachel Mimms, Ivan Liang
Designed by Yen Press Design: Wendy Chan

Yen On is an imprint of Yen Press, LLC.
The Yen On name and logo are trademarks of Yen Press, LLC.

The publisher is not responsible for websites (or their content) that are not owned by the publisher.

Library of Congress Cataloging-in-Publication Data
Names: Sato, Tsutomu. | Ishida, Kana, illustrator.
Title: The irregular at Magic High School / Tsutomu Sato ; Illustrations by Kana Ishida.
Other titles: Mahōka kōkō no rettosei. English
Description: First Yen On edition. | New York, NY : Yen On, 2016–
Identifiers: LCCN 2015042401 | ISBN 9780316348805 (v 1 : pbk.)
Subjects: CYAC: Brothers and sisters—Fiction. | Magic—Fiction. | High schools—Fiction. | Schools—Fiction. | Japan—Fiction. | Science fiction.
Classification: LCC PZ7.1.S265 Ir 2016 | DDC [Fic]—dc23
LC record available at http://lccn.loc.gov/2015042401

ISBNs: 979-8-8554-0976-5 (paperback)
979-8-8554-0977-2 (ebook)

10 9 8 7 6 5 4 3 2 1

TPA

Printed in South Korea

The Irregular at Magic High School

ESCAPE ARC II

An irregular older brother with a certain flaw.
An honor roll younger sister who is perfectly flawless.

When the two siblings enrolled in Magic High School,
it marked the beginning of tumultuous days to come—

Character

Tatsuya Shiba

Class 3-E.
Approaches everything in a detached manner. His sister Miyuki's Guardian.

Miyuki Shiba

Class 3-A. Tatsuya's younger sister; enrolled as the top student last year. Specializes in freezing magic. Dotes on her older brother.

Leonhard Saijou

Class 3-F. Tatsuya's friend. Course 2 student. Specializes in hardening magic. Has a cheerful personality.

Erika Chiba

Class 3-F. Tatsuya's friend. Course 2 student. A charming troublemaker.

Mizuki Shibata

Class 3-E. Tatsuya's friend. Has pushion-radiation sensitivity. Serious and a bit of an airhead.

Mikihiko Yoshida

Class 3-B. From a famous family who uses old magic. Has known Erika since they were children.

Honoka Mitsui

Class 3-A. Miyuki's classmate. Specializes in light-wave vibration magic. Impulsive when emotional.

Shizuku Kitayama

Class 3-A. Miyuki's classmate. Specializes in vibration and acceleration magic. Doesn't show emotional ups and downs very much.

Subaru Satomi

Class 3-D. Frequently mistaken for a pretty boy. Cheerful and easy to get along with.

Eimi "Amelia Goldie" Akechi

Class 3-B. A quarter Japanese. Almost everyone calls her "Amy." Daughter of the prominent Goldie family.

Akaha Sakurakouji

Class 3-B. Friends with Subaru and Amy. Wears gothic lolita clothes and loves theme parks.

Shun Morisaki

Class 3-A. Miyuki's classmate. Specializes in CAD quick-draw. Takes great pride in being a Course 1 student.

Hagane Tomitsuka

Class 3-E. A magic martial arts user with the nickname "Range Zero."

Mayumi Saegusa

An alum. Currently attends Magic University. Has a devilish personality but weak when on the defensive.

Azusa Nakajou

An alum. Former student council president. Shy and has trouble expressing herself.

Suzune Ichihara

An alum. Currently a student at Magic University. Calm, collected, and book smart.

Hanzou Gyoubu-Shoujou Hattori

An alum. Former head of the club committee. Gifted but can be too serious at times.

Mari Watanabe

An alum. Mayumi's good friend. Well-rounded and often sporting for a fight.

Katsuto Juumonji

An alum. Currently a student at Magic University. "A boulder-like person," according to Tatsuya.

Koutarou Tatsumi

An alum and former member of the disciplinary committee. Has a heroic and dynamic personality.

Midori Sawaki

An alum. Former member of the disciplinary committee. Has a complex about his girlish name.

Kei Isori

An alum. Former student council treasurer. Excels in magical theory. Engaged to Kanon.

Kanon Chiyoda

An alum. Former chairwoman of the disciplinary committee. As confrontational as her predecessor, Mari.

Takuma Shippou

A junior. Eldest son of the Shippou family, one of the families with excellent magicians and a new addition to the Ten Master Clans.

Minami Sakurai

A junior. Presents herself as Tatsuya and Miyuki's cousin. A Guardian candidate for Miyuki.

Isao Sekimoto

An alum and former member of the disciplinary committee. Lost the Thesis Competition. Committed acts of espionage.

Takeaki Kirihara

An alum. Junior High Kanto Kenjutsu Tournament champion.

Sayaka Mibu

An alum. Placed second in the nation at the girl's Junior High Kendo Tournament.

Kasumi Saegusa

A junior. Mayumi Saegusa's younger sister. Izumi's older twin sister. Has a cheerful and feisty personality.

Izumi Saegusa

A junior. Mayumi Saegusa's younger sister. Kasumi's younger twin sister. Has a meek and gentle personality.

Kento Sumisu

A junior. A Caucasian boy whose parents are naturalized Japanese citizens from the USNA.

Koharu Hirakawa

An alum. Participated as an engineer in the Nine School Competition. Withdrew from the Thesis Competition.

Chiaki Hirakawa

A senior. Holds enmity toward Tatsuya.

Shiina Mitsuya

A new student enrolled at First High. Always wears custom earmuffs due to her keen sense of hearing.

Saburou Yaguruma

Shiina's childhood friend and self-proclaimed bodyguard.

Haruka Ono

A general counselor of First High. Tends to get bullied but has another side to her personality.

Yakumo Kokonoe

A user of an ancient magic called *ninjutsu*. Tatsuya's martial arts master.

Satomi Asuka

First High nurse. Male students love her calm and warm smile.

Kazuo Tsuzura

First High teacher. Specializes in magic geometry. Manages the Thesis Competition team.

Jennifer Smith

A Caucasian woman naturalized as a Japanese citizen. Teaches Tatsuya's class and magic engineering classes.

Tomoko Chikura

An alum. Competed in the women's solo Shields Down, an event at the Nine School Competition.

Tsugumi Igarashi

An alum. Former biathlon club president.

Yousuke Igarashi

A senior. Tsugumi's younger brother. Has a somewhat reserved personality.

Kerry Minakami

An alum. Male representative for the main Monolith Code, an event at the Nine School Competition.

Kumiko Kunisaki

An alum. Amy's teammate in the Rower and Gunner event at the Nine School Competition. Has a frank personality.

Masaki Ichijou

A senior at Third High. Direct heir to the Ichijou family, one of the Ten Master Clans.

Shinkurou Kichijouji

A senior at Third High. Also known as Cardinal George.

Mitsugu Kuroba

Miya Shiba and Maya Yotsuba's cousin. Father of Ayako and Fumiya.

Ayako Kuroba

Tatsuya and Miyuki's second cousin. Has a younger twin brother named Fumiya. Student at Fourth High.

Fumiya Kuroba

Former candidate for the next head of the Yotsuba clan. Has an older twin sister named Ayako. Student at Fourth High.

Yoshimi

A Yotsuba magician related to the Kuroba. A psychometrist specializing in reading the psionic traces left behind in psionic information bodies. Very secretive.

Harumi Naruse

Shizuku's older cousin. Student at National Magic University Fourth Affiliated High School.

Gouki Ichijou

Masaki's father. Current head of the Ichijou family, one of the Ten Master Clans.

Midori Ichijou

Masaki's mother. Warm and good at cooking.

Akane Ichijou

Eldest Ichijou daughter. Masaki's younger sister. A junior in middle school. Likes Shinkurou.

Ruri Ichijou

Second Ichijou daughter. Masaki's younger sister. A put-together girl who marches to the beat of her own drum.

Ushio Kitayama

Shizuku's father. Big shot in the business world. His business name is Ushio Kitakata.

Benio Kitayama

Shizuku's mother. An A-rank magician who was once renowned for her vibration magic.

Wataru Kitayama

Shizuku's younger brother. Just started middle school. Dearly loves his older sister. Aims to be a magic engineer.

Toshikazu Chiba

Erika Chiba's eldest brother. Deceased. Worked at the Ministry of Police.

Naotsugu Chiba

Erika Chiba's second-eldest brother. Mari's lover. Possesses full mastery of the Chiba (thousand blades) style of kenjutsu. Nicknamed "Kirin Child of the Chiba."

Inagaki

Deceased. When he was alive, he worked as an inspector at the Ministry of Police and was Toshikazu Chiba's subordinate.

Maki Sawamura

A female actress who has been nominated for best leading female actress by distinguished movie awards. Acknowledged not only for her beauty but also her acting skills.

Pixie

A home helper robot belonging to Magic High School. Official name 3H (Humanoid Home Helper: a human-shaped chore-assisting robot) Type P94.

Ushiyama

Manager of Four Leaves Technology's CAD R&D Section 3. A person in whom Tatsuya places his trust.

Ernst Rosen

A prominent CAD manufacturer. President of Rosen Magicraft's Japanese branch.

Retsu Kudou

Renowned as the strongest magician in the world. Given the honorary title of Sage.

Makoto Kudou

Son of Retsu Kudou, elder of Japan's magic world, and current head of the Kudou family.

Minoru Kudou

Makoto's son. A junior at National Magic University Second Affiliated High School, but barely attends due to frequent illness. Also Kyouko Fujibayashi's younger brother by a different father.

Mamoru Kuki

One of the Eighteen Support Clans. Follows the Kudou family. Calls Retsu Kudou "Sensei" out of respect.

Harunobu Kazama

Commanding officer of the 101st Brigade's Independent Magic Battalion. Ranked lieutenant colonel.

Shigeru Sanada

Executive officer of the 101st Brigade's Independent Magic Battalion. Ranked major.

Kyouko Fujibayashi

Female officer serving as Kazama's aide. Ranked first lieutenant.

Hiromi Saeki

Commander of the Japan Ground Defense Force's 101st Brigade. Ranked major general. Superior officer to Harunobu Kazama, commanding officer of the Independent Magic Battalion. Due to her appearance, she is also known as the Silver Fox.

Muraji Yanagi

Executive officer of the 101st Brigade's Independent Magic Battalion. Ranked major.

Kousuke Yamanaka

Executive officer of the 101st Brigade's Independent Magic Battalion. Physician ranked major. First-rate healing magician.

Sakai

Belongs to the Japan Ground Defense Force's General Headquarters. Ranked colonel. Seen as staunchly anti–Great Asian Alliance.

Xiangshan Chen

Leader of the Great Asian Alliance Army's Special Covert Forces. Has a heartless personality.

Ganghu Lu

The ace magician of the Great Asian Alliance Army's Special Covert Forces. Also known as the "Man-Eating Tiger."

Gongjin Zhou

A handsome young man who brought Lu and Chen to Yokohama. A mysterious figure who hangs around Chinatown.

Rin

A girl Morisaki saved. Her full name is Meiling Sun. The new leader of the Hong Kong–based international crime syndicate No-Head Dragon.

Bradley Chan

A deserter of the Great Asian Alliance. Ranked first lieutenant.

Daniel Liu

A deserter of the Great Asian Alliance, like Chan. Also one of the architects of the sabotage operation in Okinawa.

Joseph Higaki

A military magician who fought the Great Asian Alliance alongside Tatsuya during the previous invasion of Okinawa. One of the Leftover Blood—descendants of orphaned children of the American soldiers who had been stationed in Okinawa.

Maya Yotsuba

Tatsuya and Miyuki's aunt. Miya's younger twin sister. The current head of the Yotsuba.

Hayama

An elderly butler employed by Maya.

Miya Shiba

Tatsuya and Miyuki's actual mother. Deceased. The only magician skilled in mental construction interference magic.

Honami Sakurai

Miya's Guardian. Deceased. Part of the first generation of the Sakura series, engineered magicians with strengthened magical capacity through genetic modification.

Sayuri Shiba

Tatsuya and Miyuki's stepmother. Dislikes them.

Yuuka Tsukuba

A candidate to become the next leader of the Yotsuba clan. Twenty-two years old. Former vice president of First High's student council. Currently a senior attending Magic University. Skilled at mental interference magic.

Katsushige Shibata

Former candidate to become the next leader of the Yotsuba clan. Employed by the Ministry of Defense. An alum of Fifth High. Specializes in convergence magic.

Kotona Tsutsumi

One of Katsushige Shibata's Guardians. A second-generation Bard series engineered magician. Specializes in sound-based magic.

Kanata Tsutsumi

One of Katsushige Shibata's Guardians. A second-generation Bard series engineered magician. Like his older sister, Kotona, he specializes in sound-based magic.

Hyougo Hanabishi

A young butler who serves the Yotsuba clan. The son of the Yotsuba clan's second butler, Hanabishi.

Angelina Kudou Shields

Commander of the USNA's magician unit, the Stars. Ranked major. Nickname is Lina. Also one of the strategic magicians called the Thirteen Apostles.

Virginia Balance

The USNA Joint Chiefs of Staff Information Bureau Internal Inspection Office's first deputy commissioner. Ranked colonel. Went to Japan in order to support Lina.

Silvia Mercury First

A planet-class magician in the USNA's magician unit, the Stars. Ranked warrant officer. Nickname is Silvie. Code name is Mercury First. During a mission in Japan, she served as Major Sirius's aide.

Benjamin Canopus

Number two in the USNA's magician unit, the Stars. Ranked major. Takes command when Major Sirius is absent.

Mikaela Hongou

An agent sent into Japan by the USNA (although she actually works as a magic scientist for the Department of Defense). Nicknamed Mia.

Claire

Hunter Q—a female soldier in Stardust, the magician unit for those who don't make it as Stars. Q refers to the 17th pursuit unit.

Alfred Fomalhaut

A first-degree star-class magician in the USNA's magician unit, the Stars. Rank is first lieutenant. Nicknamed Freddie. Currently AWOL.

Rachel

Hunter R—a female soldier in Stardust, the magician unit for those who don't make it as Stars. R refers to the 18th pursuit unit.

Charles Sullivan

A satellite-class magician in the USNA's magician unit, the Stars. Code name is Deimos Second. Currently AWOL.

Kanda

A young politician affiliated with the Civil Rights Party. Supporter of civil rights in opposition to the military. Also anti-magician.

Raymond S. Clark

A student at the high school in Berkeley, USNA, where Shizuku studies abroad. A Caucasian boy who wastes no time making advances on Shizuku. Secretly one of the Seven Sages.

Kouzuke

A young Tokyo-based politician in the ruling party. Known as a legislator with favorable views toward magicians.

Gu Jie

One of the Seven Sages. Also known as Gide Hague. A survivor of a Dahanese military's mage unit.

Kazukiyo Oumi

Known as the Dollmaker, a magic researcher who specializes in necromancy, and a practitioner of ancient magic. Rumored to use forbidden magic to reanimate corpses.

Joe Du

A mysterious man aiding Gu Jie's escape from Japan. Skilled enough at his job to consistently evade the Ten Master Clans magicians hunting them.

James Jackson

A tourist visiting Okinawa from Australia. Actually a—

Karla Schmidt

A German Union strategic magician and academic conducting research at Berlin University.

Jasmine Jackson

James's daughter. She seems no older than twelve but acts mature for her age.

Igor Andreivich Bezobrazov

A strategic magician of the New Soviet Union and leading magic researcher at the Science Academy.

William MacLeod

A British strategic magician. A prodigy who has earned several teaching accolades from universities abroad.

Edward Clark

An engineer working for the USNA National Science Agency (NSA). Administrator of Hlidskjalf.

Mai Futatsugi

Head of the Futatsugi clan, one of the Ten Master Clans. Resides in Ashiya in Hyogo Prefecture. Publicly the majority shareholder in a variety of industrial chemical- and food-processing companies. Responsible for the Hanshin and Chugoku regions.

Kouichi Saegusa

Mayumi's father and current leader of the Saegusa clan. An ultra-top-class magician.

Saburou Nakura

A powerful magician employed by the Saegusa family. Mainly serves as Mayumi's personal bodyguard.

Gen Mitsuya

Head of the Mitsuya clan, one of the Ten Master Clans. Resides in Atsugi in Kanagawa Prefecture. While it isn't exactly public knowledge, he works as an international small arms broker. Manages Lab Three, which is still operational to this day.

Isami Itsuwa

Head of the Itsuwa clan, one of the Ten Master Clans. Resides in Uwajima in Ehime Prefecture. Publicly the executive and owner of a marine-shipping company. Responsible for the Tokai, Gifu, and Nagano regions.

Atsuko Mutsuzuka

Head of the Mutsuzuka clan, one of the Ten Master Clans. Resides in Sendai in Miyagi Prefecture. Publicly the owner of a geothermal energy exploration company. Responsible for the Tohoku region.

Raizou Yatsushiro

Head of the Yatsushiro clan, one of the Ten Master Clans. Resides in Fukuoka Prefecture. Publicly a university lecturer and majority shareholder in several telecommunications companies. Responsible for all of the Kyushu region, minus Okinawa.

Kazuki Juumonji

Former head of the Juumonji clan, one of the Ten Master Clans. Resides in Tokyo. Publicly the owner of a civil engineering and construction company that primarily serves the armed forces. Shares responsibility for the Kanto region, including Izu, with the Saegusa family.

Tsukasa Tooyama

A member of the Tooyama clan, one of the Eighteen Support Clans, which aids the Ten Master Clans. The Tooyama exist to protect the functions of the state rather than the people.

Aoba Toudou

Yakumo refers to him as His Excellency, Priest Seiha. An old man with the shaved head of a priest, his origin and past are unknown. Per Yakumo, he appears to be a sponsor of the Yotsuba clan.

Glossary

Course 1 student emblem

Tatsuya Shiba's CAD

Miyuki Shiba's CAD

Magic High School
Nickname for the high schools affiliated with the National Magic University. There are nine schools throughout the nation. First High to Third High adopt a system that splits the two hundred incoming freshmen into Course 1 and Course 2 students.

Blooms, Weeds
Slang terms used at First High to express the gap between Course 1 and Course 2 students. Course 1 student uniforms sport an eight-petaled emblem on the left breast, while Course 2 student uniforms do not.

CAD (Casting Assistant Device)
A device that simplifies magic casting. Magical programming is recorded within. There are many types and forms, some specialized and others multipurpose.

Four Leaves Technology (FLT)
A domestic CAD manufacturer. Originally more famous for magical-product engineering than for developing finished products, the development of the Silver model has made FLT much more widely known in their industry.

Taurus Silver
A genius engineer said to have advanced specialized CAD software by a decade in the span of a single year.

Eidos (individual information bodies)
Originally a term from Greek philosophy. In modern magic, eidos refers to the information bodies that accompany events. They form a so-called record of those events existing in the world, and can be considered the footprints of an object's state of being in the universe, be that active or passive. The definition of magic in its modern form is that of a technology that alters events by altering the information bodies composing them.

Idea (information body dimension)
Originally a term from Greek philosophy, pronounced "ee-dee-ah." In modern magic, Idea refers to the platform upon which eidos, or information bodies, are recorded. The primary function of magic is to yield a magic program (a spell sequence) on this Idea medium and overwrite the eidos recorded there.

Activation sequence
The blueprints of magic—and the programming that constructs it. Activation sequences are stored within CADs in a compressed format. Magicians send psionic waves into the CAD, which then expands the data and uses it to convert the activation sequence into a signal. This signal returns to the magician with the decompressed magic program.

Psions (thought particles)
Massless particles belonging to the dimension of spiritual phenomena. These information particles record products of awareness and thought. Eidos are considered the theoretical basis for modern magic, while activation sequences and magic programs are the technology forming its practical basis. All of three of these bodies of information are made of psions.

Pushions (spirit particles)
Massless particles belonging to the dimension of spiritual phenomena. Their existence has been confirmed, but their true form and function have yet to be determined. In general, magicians are only able to sense energized pushions.

Magician
An abbreviation of magic technician. Refers to those with the skills to use magic at a practical level.

Magic program
An information body used to temporarily alter information connected to events. Constructed from psions possessed by magicians. Sometimes shortened to magigram.

Magic-calculation region

A mental region that constructs magic programs. The essential core of the talent of magic. Exists within the magician's unconscious regions. Though magicians can normally consciously use the magic-calculation region, they cannot perceive the processing happening within. The magic-calculation region may be called a black box, even for the magician performing the task.

Magic program output process

1. An activation sequence is transmitted to a CAD. This is called "reading an activation sequence."
2. Variables are added to the activation sequence and sent to the magic-calculation region.
3. A magic program is constructed from the activation sequence and its variables.
4. The constructed magic program is sent along the "route" from the highest part of the unconscious mind to the lowest part of the conscious mind, out the "gate" between consciousness and unconsciousness, and output to the Idea.
5. The magic program output interferes with the eidos at designated coordinates and overwrites them.

With a single-type, single-process spell, this five-stage process can be completed in under half a second. This is the bar for practical-level use with magicians.

Magic evaluation standards

The speed with which a magician constructs psionic information bodies is known as magical throughput, or processing speed. The scale and scope of the information bodies magicians can construct is known as magical capacity. The strength with which magicians overwrite eidos with magic programs is known as magical power.

Cardinal Code hypothesis

A school of thought claiming there is the existence of a total of sixteen foundational plus-and-minus magic programs within the eight types of magic—acceleration, weighting, movement, vibration, convergence, dispersion, absorption, and emission.

Typed magic

Any magic belonging to the four families and eight types.

Exotyped magic

A term for spells that control mental phenomena rather than physical ones. Encompasses many fields, from divine magic and spirit magic—which employs spiritual presences—to mind reading, astral form separation, and consciousness control.

Ten Master Clans

The most powerful magician organization in Japan. The ten families are chosen every four years from among the following twenty-eight families: Ichijou, Ichinokura, Isshiki, Futatsugi, Nikaidou, Nihei, Mitsuya, Mikazuki, Yotsuba, Itsuwa, Gotou, Itsumi, Mutsuzuka, Rokkaku, Rokugou, Roppongi, Saegusa, Shippou, Tanabata, Nanase, Yatsushiro, Hassaku, Hachiman, Kudou, Kuki, Kuzumi, Juumonji, and Tooyama.

Numbers

Just like how the Ten Master Clans contain a number from one to ten in their surnames, well-known families within the Hundred Families use numbers eleven or greater, such as Chiyoda (one thousand), Isori (fifty), and Chiba (one thousand). Although the number value is not equivalent to the family's level of strength, the presence of a number in a surname is a broad indication of that family's prominent lineage and talent.

Non-numbers

Also called Extra Numbers, or simply Extras. Magician families who have been stripped of their number. Back in the day when magicians were used as weapons and experimental subjects, success cases were given numbers, while failures—those who did not produce sufficient results—were not.

Various Spells

• Cocytus

Exotyped magic that freezes the mind. A frozen mind cannot order the flesh to die, so anyone subject to this spell enters a state of mental and physical stasis.

• Rumbling

An old spell that vibrates the ground to create a medium for an independent information body known as a spirit.

• Program Dispersion

A spell that dismantles a magic program, the main component of a spell, into a group of psionic particles with no meaningful structure. Since magic programs affect the information bodies associated with events, it is necessary for the information structure to be exposed, leaving no way to prevent interference against the magic program itself.

• Program Demolition

A typeless spell that rams a mass of compressed psionic particles directly into an object without passing through the Idea, causing it to explode and blow away the psionic information bodies recorded in magic, such as activation sequences and magic programs. Although this spell is considered a type of magic because it is a psionic bullet without any structure, such as a magic program for altering events, it is not affected by Information Boost or Area Interface. The pressure of the bullet itself also repels any Cast Jamming effects. Since it has zero physical effect, it is unblockable.

• Mine Origin

A spell that imparts strong vibrations to anything that can be conceptualized as the ground—including dirt, boulders, sand, and concrete—regardless of its composition.

• Fissure

A spell that uses independent information bodies or spirits as a medium to push a line into the ground and create a fissure in the earth.

• Dry Blizzard

A spell that gathers carbon dioxide from the air, creates dry-ice particles, then converts the extra heat energy from the freezing process to kinetic energy to launch the dry-ice particles at a high speed.

• Slithering Thunders

In addition to condensing the water vapor from Dry Blizzard's dry-ice evaporation and creating a highly conductive mist with the evaporated carbon dioxide in it, this spell creates static electricity with vibration-type magic and emission-type magic. A combination spell, it also fires an electric attack at an enemy using the carbon gas–filled mist and water droplets as a conductor.

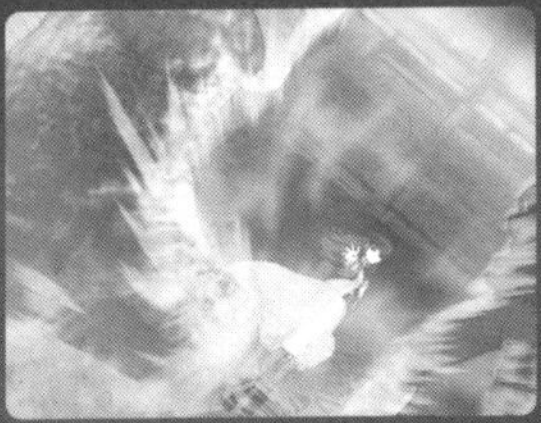

• Niflheim

A vibration- and deceleration-type area-of-effect spell. It chills a large volume of air, then moves it to freeze a wide range. In blunt terms, it creates a super-large refrigerator. The freezing white mist that appears upon activation is the particles of ice and dry ice, but at higher levels, a mist of frozen liquid nitrogen occurs.

• Burst

A dispersion-type spell that vaporizes the liquid inside a target object. When used on a creature, the spell will vaporize bodily fluids and cause the body to rupture. When used on a machine powered by internal combustion, the spell vaporizes the fuel and makes it explode. Fuel cells see the same result, and even if no combustible fuel is on board, there is no machine that does not contain some liquid, such as battery fluid, hydraulic fluid, coolant, or lubricant; once Burst activates, virtually any machine will be destroyed.

• Disheveled Hair

An old spell that, instead of specifying a direction and changing the wind's direction to that, uses air-current control to bring about the vague result of "tangling" it, causing currents along the ground that entangle an opponent's feet in the grass. Only usable on plains with grass of a certain height.

Magic Swords

Aside from fighting techniques that use magic itself as a weapon, another method of magical combat involves techniques for using magic to strengthen and control weapons. The majority of these spells combine magic with projectile weapons, such as guns and bows, but the art of the sword, known as kenjutsu, has developed in Japan as well as a way to link magic with sword techniques. This has led to magic technicians formulating personal-use magic techniques known as magic swords, which can be said to be both modern and ancient magic.

1. High-Frequency Blade

A spell that locally liquefies a solid body and cleaves it by causing a blade to vibrate at a high speed, then propagate the vibration that exceeds the molecular cohesive force of matter it comes in contact with. Used in tandem with a spell to prevent the blade from breaking.

2. Pressure Cut

A spell that generates left-right perpendicular repulsive force relative to the angle of a slashing blade edge, causing the blade to force apart any object it touches and thereby cleave it. The size of the repulsive field is less than a millimeter, but it has the strength to interfere with light, so when seen from the front, the blade edge becomes a black line.

3. Douji-Giri (Simultaneous Cut)

An ancient magic spell passed down as a secret sword art of the Genji. It is a magic sword technique wherein the user remotely manipulates two blades through a third in their hands in order to have the swords surround an opponent and slash simultaneously. *Douji* is the Japanese pronunciation for both "simultaneous" and "child," so this ambiguity was used to keep the inherited nature of the technique a secret.

4. Zantetsu (Iron Cleaver)

A secret sword art of the Chiba clan. Rather than defining a katana as a hulk of steel and iron, this movement spell defines it as a single concept, then the spell moves the katana along a slashing path set by the magic program. The result is that the katana is defined as a mono-molecular blade, never breaking, bending, or chipping as it slices through any objects in its path.

5. Jinrai Zantetsu (Lightning Iron Cleaver)

An expanded version of Zantetsu that makes use of the Ikazuchi-Maru, a personal-armament device. By defining the katana and its wielder as one collective concept, the spell executes the entire series of actions, from enemy contact to slash, incredibly quickly and with faultless precision.

6. Mountain Tsunami

A secret sword art of the Chiba clan that makes use of the Orochi-Maru, a giant personal weapon that is six feet long. The user minimizes their own inertia and that of their katana while approaching an enemy at a high speed and, at the moment of impact, adds the neutralized inertia to the blade's inertia and slams the target with it. The longer the approach run, the greater the false inertial mass, reaching a maximum of ten tons.

7. Usuba Kagerou (Antlion)

A spell that uses hardening magic to anchor a five-nanometer-thick sheet of woven carbon nanotube to a perfect surface and make it a blade. The blade that Usuba Kagerou creates is sharper than any sword or razor, but the spell contains no functions to support moving the blade, demanding technical sword skill and ability from the user.

Magic Technician Development Institutes

Laboratories for the purpose of magician development that the Japanese government established one after another in response to the geopolitical climate, which had become strained prior to World War III in the 2030s. Their objectives were not to develop magic but specifically to develop magicians, researching various methods to give birth to human specimens who were most suitable for areas of magic that were considered important, including, but not limited to, genetic engineering.

Ten magic technician development institutes were established, numbered as such, and even today, five are still in operation.

The details of each institute's research are described below.

Magic Technician Development Institute One

Established in Kanazawa in 2031. Currently shut down.

Its research focus, revolving around close combat, was the development of magic that directly manipulated biological organisms. The vaporization spell Burst is derived from this facility's research. Notably, magic that could control a human body's movements was forbidden as it enabled puppet terrorism (suicide attacks using victims that had been turned into puppets).

Magic Technician Development Institute Two

Established on Awaji Island in 2031. Currently in operation. Develops magic opposite to that of Lab One, e.g. magic that can manipulate inorganic objects, especially absorption-type spells related to oxidation-reduction reactions.

Magic Technician Development Institute Three

Established in Atsugi in 2032. Currently in operation.

With its goal of developing magicians who can react to a variety of situations when operating independently, this facility is the main driver behind the research on multicasting. In particular, it tests the limits of how many spells are possible during simultaneous casting and continual casting and develops magicians who can simultaneously cast multiple spells.

Magic Technician Development Institute Four

Details unknown. Its location is speculated to be near the old prefectural border between Tokyo and Yamanashi. Its establishment is believed to have occurred in 2033. It is assumed to be shut down, but the truth of that matter is unknown. Lab Four is rumored to be the only magic research facility that was established not only with government support but also investment from private sponsors who held strong influence over the nation; it is currently operating without government oversight and being managed directly by those sponsors. Rumors also say that those sponsors actually took over control of the facility before the 2020s.

It is said their goal is to use mental interference magic to strengthen the very wellspring of the talent called magic, which exists in a magician's unconscious—the magic-calculation region itself.

Magic Technician Development Institute Five

Established in Uwajima, Shikoku, in 2035. Currently in operation.

Researches magic that can manipulate various forms of matter. Its main focus, fluid control, is not technically difficult, but it has also succeeded in manipulating various solid forms. The fruits of its research include Bahamut, a spell jointly developed with the USNA. Along with the fluid-manipulation spell Abyss, it is known internationally as a magic research facility that developed two strategic-class spells.

Magic Technician Development Institute Six

Established in Sendai in 2035. Currently in operation. Researches magical heat control. Along with Lab Eight, it gives the impression of being a facility more for basic research than military purposes. However, it is said that they conducted the most genetic manipulation experiments out of all the magic technician development institutes, aside from Lab Four. (Though, of course, the full account of Lab Four's situation is not possible.)

Magic Technician Development Institute Seven

Established in Tokyo in 2036. Currently shut down.

Developed magic with an emphasis on anti-group combat. It successfully created colony-control magic. Contrary to Lab Six, which was largely a nonmilitary organization, Lab Seven was established as a magician development research facility that could be relied on for assistance in defending the capital in case of an emergency.

Magic Technician Development Institute Eight

Established in Kitakyushu in 2037. Currently in operation.

Researches magical control of gravitational force, electromagnetic force, strong force, and weak force. It is a pure research institute to a greater extent than even Lab Six. However, unlike Lab Six, its relationship to the JDF is steadfast. This is because Lab Eight's research focus can be easily linked to nuclear weapons development, (though they currently avoid such connotations thanks to the JDF's seal of approval).

Magic Technician Development Institute Nine

Established in Nara in 2037. Currently shut down. This facility tried to solve several problems modern magic struggled with, such as fuzzy spell manipulation, through a fusion of modern and old magic, integrating ancient knowledge into modern techniques.

Magic Technician Development Institute Ten

Established in Tokyo in 2039. Currently shut down. Like Lab Seven, doubled as capital defense, researching area magic that could create virtual structures in space as a means of defending against high-firepower attacks. It resulted in a myriad of anti-physical barrier spells.

Lab Ten also aimed to raise magic abilities through different means from Lab Four. More specifically, rather than enhancing the magic-calculation region itself, they grappled with developing magicians who responded as needed by temporarily overclocking their magic-calculation regions to use powerful magic. Whether their research was successful has not been made public.

Aside from these ten institutes, other laboratories with the goal of developing Elements were operational from the 2010s to the 2020s, but they are currently all shut down. In addition, the JDF possesses a secret research facility directly under the Ground Defense Force's General Headquarters' jurisdiction, established in 2002, which is still carrying on its research. Retsu Kudou underwent enhancement operations at this institution before moving to Lab Nine.

Strategic Magicians: The Thirteen Apostles

Because modern magic was born into a highly technological world, only a few nations were able to develop strong magic for military purposes. As a result, only a handful were able to develop "strategic-class magic," which rivaled weapons of mass destruction.

However, these nations shared the magic they developed with their allies, and certain magicians of allied nations with high aptitudes for strategic-class magic came to be known as strategic magicians.

As of April 2095, there are thirteen magicians publicly recognized as strategic-class magicians by their nations. They are called the Thirteen Apostles and are considered important players in the world's military balance. The Thirteen Apostles' nations, names, and strategic spell names are listed below.

USNA

Angie Sirius: Heavy Metal Burst
Elliott Miller: Leviathan
Laurent Barthes: Leviathan
* The only apostle belonging to the Stars is Angie Sirius. Elliott Miller is stationed at Alaska Base, and Laurent Barthes is stationed outside the country at Gibraltar Base. For the most part, their positions don't change.

New Soviet Union

Igor Andreivich Bezobrazov: Tuman Bomba
Leonid Kondratenko: Zemlja Armija
* As Kondratenko is of advanced age, he generally stays at the Black Sea Base.

Great Asian Alliance

Yunde Liu: Pilita (Thunderclap Tower)
*Yunde Liu died on October 31, 2095, in the battle against Japan.

Indo-Persian Federation

Barat Chandra Khan: Agni Downburst

Japan

Mio Itsuwa: Abyss

Brazil

Miguel Diez: Synchroliner Fusion
* This magic program was named by the USNA.

England

William MacLeod: Ozone Circle

Germany

Karla Schmidt: Ozone Circle
* Ozone Circle is based on a spell codeveloped by nations in the EU before its split as a means to fix the hole in the ozone layer. The magic program was perfected by England and then publicized to the old EU through a convention.

Turkey

Ali Sahin: Bahamut
* This magic program was developed in cooperation with the USNA and Japan, then provided to Turkey by Japan.

Thailand

Somchai Bunnag: Agni Downburst
* This magic program was provided by Indo-Persia.

The International Situation

State of the World in 2096

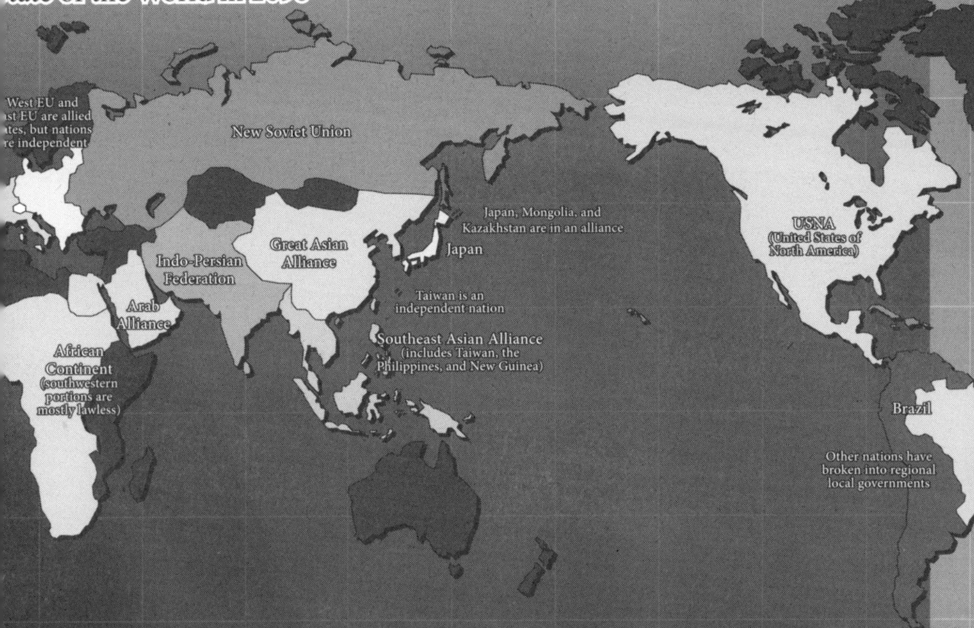

World War III, also called the Twenty Years' Global War Outbreak, was directly triggered by global cooling, and it fundamentally redrew the world map.

The USA annexed Canada and the countries from Mexico to Panama to form the United States of North America, or the USNA.

Russia reabsorbed Ukraine and Belarus to form the New Soviet Union.

China conquered northern Burma, northern Vietnam, northern Laos, and the Korean Peninsula to form the Great Asian Alliance, or GAA.

India and Iran absorbed several central Asian countries (Turkmenistan, Uzbekistan, Tajikistan, and Afghanistan) and South Asian countries (Pakistan, Nepal, Bhutan, Bangladesh, and Sri Lanka) to form the Indo-Persian Federation.

The other Asian and Arab countries formed regional military alliances to resist the three superpowers: the New Soviet Union, GAA, and the Indo-Persian Federation.

Australia chose national isolation.

The EU failed to unify and split into an eastern and a western section along the border between Germany and France. These east-west groupings also failed to properly form unions and are now actually weaker than they were before unification.

Africa saw half its nations destroyed altogether, with the surviving ones barely managing to retain urban control.

South America, excluding Brazil, fell into small, isolated states administered on a local government level.

The Irregular at Magic High School

June 9, 2097, early Sunday morning.

Exact time, 5:06 AM.

The area slightly east of the Izu Peninsula's central highlands was subjected to a large-scale, explosive magic attack. The perpetrator was presumed to be the New Soviet Union's officially recognized strategic magician Igor Andreivich Bezobrazov. His strategic magic, Tuman Bomba, likely caused the partial or complete destruction of twenty-seven private villas in the area. While there were fortunately no fatalities, eleven people sustained injuries of varying degrees.

The relatively low damage in proportion to the attack's magnitude can be attributed to the sparsely populated nature of the area and the lack of many travelers due to the current offseason. All injured persons were involved in the management of the villas.

Nevertheless, the fact remains that Japan was subjected to an unprovoked attack, posing a threat to the lives and property of its citizens. The Japanese government has immediately expressed anger to the international community against the unconfirmed attacker, without directing blame toward any particular country.

Interestingly enough, the attack was captured at close range by the National Defense Force despite the fact that it was allegedly a surprise assault occurring just after dawn. The footage, which provides solid evidence of an unjust preemptive attack, has raised suspicions that the Japanese military may have knowingly exposed its citizens to danger for diplomatic leverage by failing to act on advance knowledge of the ambush.

The National Defense Force, however, has promptly dismissed these allegations as baseless.

[1]

Miyuki screamed, frozen in shock, as soon as she saw Minami collapsed on the dining room floor. Luckily, her panic was short-lived. It didn't take her long to become mobile again, although she was still filled with terror.

"Minami!" she cried, rushing over.

Pixie already had two fingers on Minami's wrist, checking her pulse. Miyuki dropped to her knees and put her hand near Minami's nose. Her shoulders drooped in slight relief when she felt a sign of breathing. But then she touched Minami's neck, and her complexion turned pale.

"She's cold," she whispered. "And her pulse is weak. Tatsuya, please! Do something!"

She gazed up pleadingly at her brother. Though she hadn't been there when Honami died, it was as if she were reenacting the trauma of Minami's mother's all-too-similar death. Tatsuya, too, found it hard to hide his concern.

"How is she doing, Pixie?" he asked the robot with a tremor in his voice.

"No sign of external injuries, Master," Pixie replied telepathically. *"However, her temperature, blood pressure, and pulse are all at dangerous levels. At this rate, there is a high chance of her vitals deteriorating until she succumbs."*

Tatsuya usually forbade Pixie from using telepathy without permission. But he was so frustrated with the situation that this small act of rebellion didn't set him off. There was no time for that. Tatsuya raised his empty left hand toward Minami. His right hand still firmly grasped the large CAD Trident pistol, which he had used for Mist Dispersion, but he had neither time nor presence of mind to use it to cast Regenerate. He didn't even have the mental capacity to retrieve the regeneration spell's storage.

Instead, he cast Regenerate using nothing but his own power.

Eidos-based regeneration involved tracing the body's history of changes and copying the eidos of the desired physical state—usually one without damage—to overwrite the current eidos. Events came with information. Therefore, when someone rewrote the information of those events, they changed accordingly.

In other words, changing information altered events. This was the essence of modern magic. The information of an event—the eidos—has an inherent tendency to restore itself and artificially altered eidos would, over time, gradually revert to their original state, thus making magic alterations impermanent.

On the other hand, past eidos were simply the information bodies that were associated with past events. As long as there were no contradictions in information, there would be no reversion, only whatever changes would have naturally occurred over time.

Subjects that had their eidos rewritten with their own past eidos would be perfectly restored to that past state, with the caveat that they would experience the passage of time without external influence, from that moment in the past until the present. In other words, regeneration magic traced back to the proper time of an event and, after isolating for that event, restored the world to that moment in the past. Rather than altering the *effects* of the injuries like conventional magic, Tatsuya's regeneration magic addressed the *cause*.

Tatsuya aimed his spell directly at Minami, processing her physical information and reviewing its change history. Yet he couldn't find the root of her deteriorating condition.

Then he processed the psion information bodies associated with Minami's body and traced their change history. The cause was still nowhere to be found.

Tatsuya dived deeper. He processed the psion information bodies that connected Minami's mind and body, going through their change history.

This used to be a difficult task for him. He couldn't have done it back when Honami overheated her magic-calculation region five years ago, or even one month ago.

Accessing psion information bodies was easy enough, but retrieving the information was another matter. And fully deciphering the structural information was a challenge for any magician. This time, however, Tatsuya could do it.

Now that he was free from Oath, Tatsuya had regained his full power. His access to Material Burst wasn't the only thing that had changed; the scope of his eidos regeneration spell had expanded as well.

He could now retrace and duplicate the structural information of psion information bodies—or ethereal bodies, which directly connected to the mind. However, even with this newfound ability, the fundamental cause of Minami's deterioration remained a mystery. There were clearly still some flaws in the composition of her ethereal bodies.

Localized information loss had caused several cavities to form within the bodies, much like moths chewing holes into clothing. But this wasn't the cause of Minami's worsening condition; it was the result, which directly affected her body's ability to restore itself. Repairing the holes wouldn't address the fundamental issue unless these restoration abilities were fixed.

Unfortunately, if the damage to the information bodies of the mind was left untreated for too long, those of the body, as well as Minami's physical condition, would continue to deteriorate.

Ethereal bodies sent commands from the mind to the body. And damaged ethereal bodies transmitted damaged information. The body misinterpreted these commands as instructions from the mind to break itself down. As a result, the body would begin to decay even if it was physically fine. This was why, even if it wasn't a perfect solution, immediate action was crucial.

Thankfully, Tatsuya's regeneration spell managed to revive Minami's psion information bodies.

The spell overwrote the structures of both the psion information bodies associated with her body and those connecting her body and mind with structural information from before the attack. Once the renewed past information underwent automatic adjustments to account for the passage of time, the eidos became fixed in the present.

"*Body temperature has risen to thirty-five degrees Celsius. Blood pressure and heart rate are no longer at dangerous levels*," Pixie reported telepathically.

Yet there was still no sign of Minami regaining consciousness.

"Pixie, get a futon for Minami to lie on," Tatsuya ordered.

"*Yes, Master*," the robot replied, springing into action.

Tatsuya then turned to Miyuki. "Warm the area around Minami to match her current body temperature."

"All right!" Miyuki nodded and immediately cast a spell to interfere with the temperature of the floor and the air.

Before she had finished, Tatsuya rushed to the phone. His goal was not to call emergency services but to contact the Yotsuba main house.

"*Can I help you, Master Tatsuya?*" Hayama asked on the other end of the line.

Despite the early hour, the butler was already dressed impeccably in his uniform. Tatsuya, on the other hand, was still in his pajamas. He didn't have time to dwell on that, and Hayama thankfully didn't show any sign of reproach. But Tatsuya decided to apologize anyway.

"Sorry for my appearance," Tatsuya began. "The villa was attacked with long-range magic. I think it was Tuman Bomba."

Hayama's eyebrows lifted in mild surprise. "*Are you all right?*" he asked with a hint of tension.

"Miyuki and I are completely unharmed. Minami, on the other hand, has collapsed from her magic-calculation region overheating. We gave her emergency care, but she should see a professional as soon as possible."

Hayama paled slightly. Though his agitation lasted only a moment, it was a sign that the Yotsuba clan's senior members couldn't ignore mention of the magic-calculation region overheating. Especially since it was suspected to be the cause of death of the former clan head, Genzou Yotsuba.

"*I understand,*" Hayama said, nodding. "*We will arrange for her hospitalization immediately. Hyougo should be there in a matter of minutes.*"

"Thank you."

Having completed his objective, Tatsuya hung up.

◇ ◇ ◇

A group of Tsukuba clan magicians had used mental interference magic to establish a barrier within approximately a one-kilometer radius around the villa where Tatsuya was staying. This barrier was a defensive mechanism to repel both magicians and regular humans who lacked resistance to mental interference magic. It also served as a sensor that alerted the spell caster if anyone managed to infiltrate the area.

A particular armored vehicle with a camouflage exterior and variable suspension had snuck its way through the barrier without detection the previous night. Though it was unmistakably a military vehicle, the Tsukuba clan magicians had yet to notice its presence. What made things even more curious was that the vehicle had traveled on public roads, and yet there had been no mention of it on social media or other public platforms.

By lowering its variable suspension earlier that morning, the armored vehicle had survived Tuman Bomba's blast. Four military personnel sat inside.

"The psion sensors are not detecting anything new. The long-range magic attacks seem to have ceased," one of the personnel reported to the commander of the Independent Magic Battalion's 101st Brigade, who was sitting in the front passenger seat.

"I see," Lieutenant Colonel Kazama responded without looking back.

Kazama's behavior wasn't due to laziness. In fact, many would have considered it normal to treat his subordinates this way, given his position. The real reason he didn't look back was because he was preoccupied with something else.

His eyes half closed, the lieutenant colonel sat with his back straight and both hands frozen in mudra-like gestures. He had been like this for hours, not only since the armored vehicle had parked but on its journey to Izu as well. As if unaffected by the shaking and vibration of the vehicle, Kazama remained perfectly aligned with the earth's gravity.

The reason the Tsukuba clan magicians had not sensed the armored vehicle enter the barrier was thanks to Kazama's eerie pose. He used it to cast a perception inhibition spell—the tengu technique, Cloak of Concealment. This spell made others see without truly seeing and hear without truly hearing. In other words, instead of blocking light or sound waves, it interfered with people's consciousness, making them believe a physical object wasn't actually there.

It was precisely this tengu technique that had defeated the Tsukuba clan barrier and prevented the Tsukuba clan magicians from recognizing that their barrier had been breached. Despite Kazama's formidable abilities, which had earned him the nickname "Great

Tengu," fooling Yotsuba magicians wasn't an easy task. The lieutenant colonel's focus was so intense and unwavering because he didn't have the luxury to do anything else.

"Withdraw," Kazama ordered curtly.

"Yes, sir," the personnel replied. "Observations complete. Prepare to withdraw."

Each member of the team retrieved the media-recording data from their assigned observation equipment and stored it in protective cases.

Then, one after the other, they announced, "Preparation for withdrawal complete."

"Raising the vehicle," the driver said.

He promptly lifted the armored vehicle's suspension and switched it to off-road driving mode.

"Preparation for withdrawal complete," he announced.

Seconds later, the vehicle's external microphone picked up the sound of an approaching motor.

◇ ◇ ◇

The barrier around the villa where Tatsuya was staying was managed by a rotating group of Tsukuba clan magicians located in a small hut. This particular day just so happened to be the shift of Tsukuba clan heiress, Yuuka.

The prior evening, the Tsukuba clan hadn't deemed it necessary for their heiress to keep an all-night watch. Awakened by the intense magic waves caused by Tuman Bomba's attack, Yuuka rushed into the control room in her pajamas and robe.

"Status report! Now!"

The young male magicians at the control panel stiffened at the heiress's casual appearance. Her modest, girl-next-door sleepwear made them all blush. Yet their response remained calm.

"Almost everything aboveground was destroyed," one magician reported.

The only reason he could maintain such a detached tone was because both the hut's bedroom and its control room were constructed underground. The surveillance hut aboveground was not for monitoring the villa itself but those who approached the villa. This allowed the underground portion to function as the main structure, while the area aboveground served as camouflage.

"What was the cause?" Yuuka pressed.

The surge of magic energy that had jolted her awake was enough to give her a good idea of what had happened. She only posed the question in case she had missed something in her groggy state.

"It was an extremely powerful long-range magic attack," another magician explained. "It caused an airborne explosion with largely controlled shock waves."

"Were the shock waves controlled by magic?" Yuuka asked, confused.

"No, it seems the caster used a containment barrier to control them," the magician answered.

"Interesting," Yuuka murmured.

She didn't fully understand how this worked, but there was only one type of magic capable of such power and control.

"Was the attack Tuman Bomba?" she asked.

"Most likely," a magician replied.

"How are Tatsuya and Miyuki?"

"The villa is untouched, so they are probably safe," another magician answered.

A doubtful frown appeared on Yuuka's face. She didn't think it was strange that Tatsuya and Miyuki were safe, but she couldn't believe the villa had escaped damage entirely.

"Wasn't Tatsuya's villa at the center of the attacks?" she asked.

"Yes, but a powerful shield protected it."

Yuuka turned to her new Guardian, Chiho Ouzaki. "What do you make of that?"

"It was probably Minami," Chiho replied without hesitation.

Chiho, too, was an augmented magician of the Sakura series. But unlike Honami and Minami Sakurai, she was born from a separate fertilized egg, essentially forming the second generation of a different lineage. Eight years older than Minami, Chiho had an understated appearance that made her look like an ordinary office worker despite being a magician.

Chiho's specialty magic also followed the rules of the Sakura series. Her strongest spell produced a shield dedicated to object and heat defense. While this shield was best at individualized heat protection, it could also provide versatile defense against physical objects and energy sources.

Chiho reasoned that if the attack's shock waves had been scattered, Tatsuya's disassembly magic was involved. If they were weakened, Miyuki's vibration deceleration magic was the logical culprit. Since Minami specialized in defense magic, she was the likeliest of the three to cast a magic shield.

"Could you have produced the same kind of shield?" Yuuka asked.

Her blunt question didn't seem to bother Chiho, who replied, "Probably, but..."

"But what?"

Chiho hesitated for a moment before continuing.

"I don't think I could do much more after that. Stopping such a powerful force would inevitably make my magic-calculation region overheat, and I would lose consciousness."

Yuuka paled. As the Yotsuba clan's magic-calculation region specialist and doctor, she was particularly knowledgeable about damage to the magic-calculation region caused by overheating. Minami may not be her own bodyguard, but Yuuka still couldn't overlook the potential of serious mental injury.

"I'll be ready in five minutes," she told Chiho. "Meet me at the car."

"Should I help you get dressed?"

One glance at the Tsukuba clan heiress must have made Chiho think that getting ready in five minutes would be a challenge. Unlike Yuuka, who was still in her pajamas, Chiho was fully dressed in a crisp pantsuit.

"No, thank you," Yuuka responded curtly and returned to her room.

Meanwhile, Chiho quickly made her way to the garage, so she was ready to depart at a moment's notice.

Since it was aboveground, the garage had been destroyed by the Tuman Bomba attack. Luckily, its intentionally simplistic design spared any vehicles from being buried under debris.

Yuuka climbed into an off-road car with the appearance of a commercial SUV and the defense of an armored vehicle. As she was making herself comfortable, it suddenly occurred to her to check the status of the barrier around the villa.

She gasped. "What in the world?"

Chiho refrained from immediately keying the ignition and turned to Yuuka. "Is something wrong?"

"We have an intruder," Yuuka replied.

"Did the barrier fail to detect their presence?" Chiho asked calmly, helping Yuuka regain her composure.

"No. This is a terrible oversight on our part. I'm worried about Minami, but this takes priority."

Chiho didn't fight back.

"I can call for the emergency deployment of the entire staff," she suggested.

"Please do. But we'll go on ahead," Yuuka said, only partially taking her Guardian's advice.

"All right."

Chiho started the off-road car at Yuuka's signal and began driving in the designated direction. She knew her barrier magic was strong enough to hold off the intruders until reinforcements arrived. The target's vehicle was positioned at a ninety-degree angle from the center of the villa. Its camouflaged, angular form immediately gave its identity away.

"That's a military armored vehicle," Chiho noted.

Yuuka wasn't as well versed in cars as Chiho, but even she could see it was special.

"I want to speak to whoever is inside," she said. "Park directly in front of it."

Chiho obediently parked the off-road car directly in the armored vehicle's path.

"We should probably wait for reinforcements," she suggested.

"I agree." Yuuka followed her Guardian's advice and patiently stayed in the car.

◇ ◇ ◇

As soon as the small SUV parked in front of their armored vehicle, the driver turned to Kazama for instructions.

"What should we do, Colonel?" he asked.

Kazama released his hand mudras and reached for the door. "All of you stay in the car. Don't do anything to make them think we're hostile."

He stepped out of the armored vehicle and faced the SUV in a way that made his actions completely visible. He knew he was being observed. Once completely out in the open, he stopped and waited for a response.

For a while, nothing happened, and Kazama immediately knew why. The area they were in was relatively exposed. Kazama had intentionally chosen it to record the attack on the villa. The view, however, was partially obscured by trees. Kazama detected people hidden in his blind spots. Eleven, to be exact. He could sense they were all skilled magicians—clearly reinforcements.

The SUV's two front doors opened simultaneously. A young woman stepped out and spoke loud and clear. Kazama was about five meters away, and the wind was blowing, but he had no trouble hearing her.

"I'm Yuuka Tsukuba, the eldest daughter of the Yotsuba clan's Tsukuba branch," she announced. "You must be the commanding officer of the 101st Brigade's Independent Magic Battalion, Lieutenant Colonel Kazama."

If this woman was who she said she was, it wouldn't be surprising for her to know who Kazama was. He remained unfazed.

"That's correct," he replied without moving from the side of his vehicle.

He had a feeling Yuuka didn't want him to approach, but the young woman surprised him by walking toward him. Kazama quickly followed suit to meet her in the middle.

The move on his part was to some extent meant as a display of confidence. But that wasn't all. He was also worried that making a young woman walk all the way over to him could signal fear to his subordinates.

The woman who had been sitting in the SUV's driver's seat followed closely behind Yuuka. Kazama guessed her failure to take the lead was proof of her confidence in defensive magic.

That must be Miss Tsukuba's Guardian, Kazama thought. *I can tell she's experienced.*

Tatsuya had told him a little about Yotsuba clan Guardians. The woman at Yuuka's heels exuded an aura that gave her position away. While Kazama was briefly absorbed with Chiho, Yuuka had approached close enough to engage in conversation.

"Colonel Kazama," she said. "As you may very well know, you are currently on Yotsuba private property. Technically, it's owned by a real estate company that the Yotsuba clan controls, but that's beside the point. What I mean to say is, what is the National Defense Force doing on private property? Especially in something like that."

Yuuka glanced at the armored vehicle.

It was a logical question, but Kazama wasn't sure how to respond. Since he had not expected anyone to discover them, he didn't have any excuses prepared. It was a stroke of bad luck that the Tuman Bomba incident had aligned perfectly with Yuuka's shift. If any other magician had been in charge, Kazama would have gone undetected.

Unfortunately, the fact remained that Yuuka had caught him. Kazama didn't make a habit of being overconfident, but he had clearly underestimated the Tsukuba clan magicians' skill. He took this as a lesson and vowed to be more cautious in the future.

Failing to come up with a convincing excuse, he resorted to a weak attempt at downplaying the situation.

"I'm not at the liberty to divulge confidential military information," he said.

"Does that confidential information have anything to do with knowledge of a foreign attack on civilians?" Yuuka countered.

Unfortunately for Kazama, she was not intimidated by military clout. She turned back to Chiho.

"From the looks of it, that armored vehicle seems to be equipped for surveillance. Wouldn't you agree?"

"Definitely. That looks like recon equipment to me," the Guardian responded with a tone not quite as definitive as her statement.

"Please don't misunderstand," Kazama said defensively but calmly. "We're not here as enemies of the Yotsuba clan."

"Are you saying the members of the Yotsuba clan are not civilians?" Yuuka asked.

She was keen enough to pick up on Kazama's implication. But this was exactly what Kazama wanted.

"Well, formalities aside, it's fair to say the members of the Yotsuba clan are not strictly civilians," he said to Yuuka.

"Why put formalities aside when they're crucial to the definition of public servants?"

There was a moment of hesitation in her rebuttal, however. She couldn't completely deny what Kazama claimed, and she knew it.

"Would you prefer I reinstate those formalities, then?" Kazama asked with a faint smile.

Yuuka faltered.

"I'm more interested in knowing whether the military anticipated the Tuman Bomba attack."

These confrontational words came not from Yuuka but from the shadows of the trees. Kazama spun with a panic on his face that was impossible to hide.

"Tatsuya...," he and Yuuka whispered in unison.

◇ ◇ ◇

"Is something wrong, Tatsuya?" Miyuki asked from Minami's side.

She looked up at her brother, the tension on his face obvious. Minami was stable for now. Her unconscious state still made the situation uncertain, but at least her condition was not as critical as it had been a few moments prior.

Tatsuya had just changed out of his pajamas into casual clothes to meet the helicopter that would take Minami to the hospital. When he returned to the dining room, he was still concerned but not particularly anxious. Then, a few seconds later, he suddenly became fully alert, as if an enemy was close by. Miyuki couldn't tell what had triggered this change.

"Colonel Kazama is here," Tatsuya said.

Miyuki gasped with embarrassment. "He is?! I had no idea..."

"Neither did I," Tatsuya admitted. "Yuuka's magic must have brought him out of hiding."

"Yuuka is here, too?"

"Yeah, Tsukuba clan magicians make sure no one comes near the villa," Tatsuya explained. "Probably under Aunt Maya's orders."

"Aunt Maya…"

Miyuki looked puzzled; she was unsure whether Maya was doing this out of kindness for Tatsuya. But there was no point in her speculating about their aunt's true intentions now. Guessing wouldn't do her much good, even if it ended up unveiling the truth. Before Miyuki stepped into a meaningless maze, Tatsuya brought her back to reality and the issue at hand.

"I'm going out to meet the colonel," he said. "Stay here with Minami."

When Tatsuya arrived at the armored vehicle, he found Kazama and Yuuka in the middle of a heated discussion. He gestured to silence the Tsukuba clan magicians who had noticed his arrival, and he blended into the scenery to eavesdrop.

If Yuuka and Kazama hadn't been so engaged in conversation, they would have immediately detected Tatsuya. But luckily enough, both of them were too wary of each other as mental interference magicians to pay much attention to anything else.

Tatsuya was especially surprised by Kazama's low guard, given his reputation as the Great Tengu. While the lieutenant colonel would never admit it, the fatigue of single-handedly contending with the Tsukuba clan magicians' barrier had clearly taken its toll.

"*Does that confidential information have anything to do with knowledge of a foreign attack on civilians?*" Yuuka asked.

Her comment sent ripples through Tatsuya's mind. He could tell that Kazama's armored vehicle was equipped more for recon than for combat. Moreover, its expensive equipment hinted it was here to gather valuable data.

Is Yuuka right? Tatsuya thought. *Did the National Defense Force know about the Tuman Bomba attacks in advance?*

If this was true, he couldn't let it slide.

"*Would you prefer I reinstate those formalities then?*" Kazama remarked smugly.

Yuuka fell silent. Realizing there wasn't much time to spare, Tatsuya decided to abandon his post as a bystander.

"I'm more interested in knowing whether the military anticipated the Tuman Bomba attack," he said, stepping out of the shadows.

"Tatsuya...," Kazama and Yuuka whispered simultaneously.

"Would you mind enlightening us, Colonel?" Tatsuya asked.

He didn't bother to salute or even greet Kazama. Nothing bothered him more than dulling his own wit through the exchange of friendly greetings.

"As I said to Miss Tsukuba earlier, I'm not at the liberty to divulge confidential military information," Kazama replied hesitantly.

"Can I take that as a yes?" Tatsuya challenged.

"No comment," Kazama said.

Tatsuya sighed, his gaze fixed on the lieutenant colonel.

"I feel like I owe you a debt of gratitude and I respect you, so it pains me to say this so bluntly," he began. "But if you had warned me in advance, it would have saved me from the surprise of the New Soviet Union's attack."

"......"

Kazama was silent for a moment before speaking again.

"Are you certain that long-range attack came from the New Soviet Union?"

Though the lieutenant colonel was clearly intrigued, Tatsuya was concerned by something else entirely.

"Would some concrete evidence relieve your doubts?" the high schooler asked.

Kazama had a sneaking suspicion that the New Soviet Union's strategic magician who was one of the Thirteen Apostles was responsible for the attack earlier that morning, but he couldn't be sure. Tatsuya, on the other hand, was now 100 percent positive that Kazama had known about the long-range magic attack in advance.

Any evidence that Tatsuya could provide would make it completely clear that the New Soviet Union was behind the surprise attack. Kazama realized that Tatsuya's knowledge was worth enough to disclose his own information and level the playing field.

"...I believe it would," the lieutenant colonel replied.

"The magic used in the surprise attack was cast at a railroad near Vladivostok," Tatsuya began.

"A railroad?" Kazama echoed.

"Yes." Tatsuya nodded. "I reached this conclusion based on the information gathered from the magic user I believe cast the Tuman Bomba spell."

"So you've captured Bezobrazov?!" Yuuka exclaimed in surprise.

"I defeated the two magicians behind the spell, but they weren't Bezobrazov," Tatsuya replied. "In fact, both of them were women."

"Two women?!" Yuuka exclaimed again.

"They must be undisclosed strategic magicians," Kazama murmured astutely.

"I don't believe Bezobrazov was completely uninvolved, but the magicians I encountered were those two women," said Tatsuya. "And they were definitely in the Far Eastern territories of the New Soviet Union."

"If they were attacking from rail tracks, they may have been in a private train car on the New Siberian Railroad," Kazama mused.

This was a significant revelation for the National Defense Force. There were theories that the activation of Tuman Bomba required a CAD large enough to occupy an entire train car, but they lacked substantial evidence. When a spell resembling Tuman Bomba was cast near the Soya Strait, there were no reports of train movement. This left the National Defense Force confused and wondering whether the train theory was false or if the magic used near the Soya Strait was an entirely different spell altogether.

Now, Tatsuya's testimony proved that at least the train element was real. Although he was still unsure whether the surprise attack spell was Tuman Bomba, it most likely was, judging from its power and range. If it wasn't Tuman Bomba, that would mean the New

Soviet Union possessed another immensely powerful spell capable of striking at ultra–long range.

Either way, the fact remained that a spell capable of threatening Japan had been unleashed from a private train car. The military's capacity for surveillance was limited, but once a target was identified, resources to track it could be effectively allocated. Before Kazama could bask in the satisfaction of receiving such valuable information, Tatsuya brought him back to reality.

"Now it's your turn, Colonel," Tatsuya said.

Right, Kazama thought.

Tatsuya's information didn't come for free. They had made a deal.

"So tell me," Tatsuya continued. "Did the National Defense Force know there would be a surprise attack here this morning?"

"We weren't certain," Kazama replied. "Even if an attack was planned, we didn't know when."

"But you *did* predict the attack would land here. How?"

Kazama found it difficult to answer right away, since it would reveal the military's intelligence-gathering capabilities. He was unsure whether he had the authority to disclose such information despite or perhaps *because* of Tatsuya's loose affiliation with the National Defense Force.

Rather than waiting for Kazama's response, Tatsuya continued.

"Did the National Defense Force, or rather, Major General Saeki, obtain information on Bezobrazov's movements? Is that how they predicted the surprise attack?"

Kazama remained silent. This reaction was enough for Tatsuya to realize his hypothesis was correct.

If he had received warning of the surprise attack in advance, Minami wouldn't have collapsed, he wouldn't have let Miyuki and Minami to come to the villa, and even if he did get hit by the attack, he knew he wouldn't have suffered any lasting injuries. Despite the urge to say some choice words, Tatsuya swallowed it down. He knew there was no point in venting his resentment at Kazama.

"Anyway," Tatsuya said, "I have an injured person to deal with back at the villa. Yuuka, Colonel, I'll see you later."

"Wait!" Yuuka called out from behind Tatsuya. "Is it Minami who's injured?"

"That's right," Tatsuya replied. "You can probably guess the state she's in."

Minami didn't have any external wounds. It was her magic-calculation region—a part of her psyche—that had suffered damage. Yuuka had already guessed this was the case, but it was still hard for her to hide her worry.

"We have to get her to a hospital!" she exclaimed. "Can I do anything to help?"

"The main house already has a helicopter on its way. It should get here at any minute, so I should go," Tatsuya replied.

"O-oh… Well…," Yuuka stammered. "I hope she'll be okay."

"Thank you," Tatsuya said.

He gave both Yuuka and Kazama a quick nod before walking away. Yuuka stared anxiously at his receding back, while Kazama remained silent.

[2]

The hospital where Minami was admitted was very close to Miyuki's Chofu residence. This was, of course, no coincidence. The apartment building was constructed as the Yotsuba family's Tokyo base with the potential need to care for the injured in mind.

Tatsuya and Miyuki were back at the new apartment. Miyuki had wanted to stay at the hospital with Minami, but the doctor had gently denied her request. His reasoning was that the magic Miyuki exuded would interfere with the hospital's treatment. Miyuki obviously couldn't argue otherwise.

She huddled next to Tatsuya on the Chofu living room couch.

"I hope Minami is all right," she whispered, both unable and unwilling to hide her worry.

"Her wounds shouldn't be fatal," Tatsuya said.

This was exactly what Miyuki wanted to hear. Her face regained some of its color.

"You're right," she said, nodding. "The regeneration spell you cast on her should have put her in the clear."

Tatsuya gave her an uncertain glance. He hated to fuel her anxiety, but he also felt it unfair to simply soothe her with comforting words.

"All I did was some rudimentary first aid," Tatsuya admitted. "I couldn't heal her completely." Before Miyuki's unease could rear its head again, he added, "But I did manage to stabilize her physical condition before it became life-threatening. Besides, Minami is a second-generation Sakurai. Her magic defenses should be much stronger than a first-generation Sakurai, like Honami."

"That's true!" Miyuki quickly perked up, her eyes desperately searching her brother's. "Magic becomes more ingrained in our genetic makeup each generation. That should apply to engineered magicians like us as well."

Tatsuya felt a tinge of resentment at Miyuki's choice of words.

"Well...yes," he conceded. "Typically, the second generation of engineered magicians is more stable than the first. There are a few exceptions, but that's the usual trend."

Generally speaking, engineered magicians were unstable organisms. There were even instances where they suddenly weakened and died. Some passed away without any warning at all.

There was still no explanation for this, but several hypotheses had been proposed. The most compelling one in Tatsuya's opinion was the theory of psychic-limiter failure. This suggested that engineered magicians wielded magic without any mental limiters to speak of.

The human mind wasn't naturally equipped for magic. While magic-calculation regions were an inherent part of all human minds, casting magic imposed a burden on the mind beyond what it could handle. Therefore, under regular circumstances, limiters in the unconscious mind capped magic use to a solid 100 percent.

In rare cases, individuals with strong mental endurance against magic had limiters that were more forgiving. These individuals were usually born with limiters set around 99 to 98 percent. Although only 1 or 2 percent lower than the norm, there was a significant difference between having some leeway and having none.

Just like muscle, the magic-calculation region's output increased the more it was used. As bones and tendons toughened to support increased muscle, the mind also built endurance with regular magic use. Some argued that this led to the simultaneous release of limiters in the magic-calculation region and the enhancement of magic output.

In other words, regular magicians gradually enhanced their endurance against magic by both using it and increasing the release of their limiters. Engineered magicians, on the other hand, had been artificially induced to use magic. Due to the lack of natural limiter functions, it was believed that they could easily suffer from limiter failure.

Exposure to magic beyond a magician's mental endurance threshold eventually led to damage, which then affected the body's vital functions. This would explain why engineered magicians were so unstable and prone to sudden injury or death.

Specialists believed that mental endurance against magic was an acquired trait. Neo-Lamarckism, which advocated for the inheritance of acquired physical traits, was not a part of mainstream evolutionary theory. Yet in the field of mental adaptation to magic, the very inheritance of acquired traits that Neo-Lamarckism proposed most effectively explained magic's genetically ingrained phenomenon.

If the notion—sometimes referred to as psychological Lamarckism—was true, then second-generation magicians inherently possessed an endurance against magic that the first generation acquired as they met their own destruction. The third generation then inherited an even stronger endurance from the second generation.

This was all speculation, of course, so there was no guarantee that it was true. However, it did seem that Minami, as a second-generation engineered magician, was more resilient against the excessive use of magic than first-generation Honami. For Miyuki, this came as a slight relief, and the signs of anxiety faded from her face.

At the same time, she still harbored a significant sense of guilt at the thought that Minami had sacrificed herself for her sake. Tatsuya sensed Miyuki's feelings on the matter and gave her a smile, hiding his own concerns.

He struggled to come to terms with the fact that Miyuki was an engineered magician. He would prefer not to believe it, but he lacked the grounds to say it was completely untrue. It wasn't that he was averse to engineered magicians, but the thought that Miyuki may have been manipulated by someone—even if it happened before she was born—upset him to no end. He was not completely conscious of these feelings, which bordered on possessiveness.

Emotions aside, if Tatsuya were to accept Miyuki as an engineered magician, he would inevitably have to face a series of grave concerns. Among them was something Maya had mentioned before—whether Miyuki had truly overcome the intrinsic instability of the Yotsuba clan.

Maya's words alone were proof that Miyuki was indeed an engineered magician. On the other hand, Miyuki's limiters functioned normally. It was also possible that she possessed such a high innate resistance against magic that her limiters were unnecessary. Tatsuya had no way to verify this. Even now that he was completely free from Oath, his power couldn't extend to the cerebral realm. At this point, he had no choice but to believe what he was told.

Of course, it was still possible that Miyuki was a flawed engineered magician. One day, she could meet the fate of all engineered magicians before her and die suddenly. Tatsuya couldn't imagine a future beyond that. He might not even have the strength to live. Either way, one thing was clear: He didn't have the confidence to handle that potential destiny entirely on his own.

◇ ◇ ◇

At 2 PM Japan time, the Japanese government expressed its anger to the international community without identifying a specific party. But it had already become common knowledge that a powerful magical reaction was detected in the New Soviet Union's Far East territory while Japan's Izu Peninsula was under attack. No one within the USNA government or military failed to connect these two events.

Lina was informed of the situation several hours later. It was still

Saturday, June 8, at the Stars headquarters in New Mexico, USNA. A meeting was held after routine training that evening to brief Lina and other senior Stars military officers on the shocking news. Commander Walker announced that a region of Japan near the capital was subjected to a New Soviet Union strategic-magic attack shortly before midnight, local time.

"Furthermore," he continued, "we believe the target of the attack was Tatsuya Shiba, the newly identified Japanese strategic magician."

"How is Tatsuya Shiba now?"

It wasn't Lina who posed this question. She was still in shock and having trouble thinking straight. Instead, it was Canopus who had spoken.

A deputy officer turned to Walker for confirmation before responding.

"We have yet to receive a detailed report, but he is alive and well as far as we know."

A wave of mixed reactions spread across the room. Lina was obviously relieved; Canopus with his tightly drawn lips seemed to be wondering whether Tatsuya would retaliate; Arcturus displayed a hint of disappointment that the assassination mission would not be canceled; Vega, though on the same mission, wore a defiant smile, happy that she still had a chance to kill Tatsuya with her own hands.

"The USNA Joint Chiefs of Staff have ordered us to adopt a basic noninterference stance in regard to this incident," Walker said. "I doubt any of you will be asked to make a public statement, but please keep this in mind."

Everyone nodded. Lina wasn't the only one in the room unhappy with this decision, but they all understood it was not their place to speak up.

"Dismissed."

At Walker's signal, the USNA's top thirteen magicians saluted simultaneously. As they filed out of the room with Lina at the lead, Walker called out to the group.

"Captain Arcturus, could you stay behind, please?"

It was standard protocol for all orders to go through Lina, who was commander of the Stars. At the same time, it wasn't uncommon for orders to be issued without her consent. This time was no exception, and Lina wasn't bothered.

She exited with the other team commanders and deputy officers, leaving Walker and Arcturus alone. The briefing room they were in was equipped with a robust counterespionage system, which was, of course, currently operational.

"Set up a soundproof field, Captain," Walker ordered.

"Yes, sir."

With a skeptical expression, Arcturus obediently blocked all sound both in and out of the room.

"The field is up, sir," he announced.

Since Walker wasn't a magician, he couldn't verify Arcturus's claim for himself. Nonetheless, he replied with a reassured "Good" and proceeded to say, "The specifics for the experiment have been decided."

A look of unease crossed Arcturus's face. "You mean the micro black hole experiment?" he whispered.

Despite the soundproof field, he felt the need to lower his voice.

"That's right." Walker nodded. "It will be held in the same place as before—Dallas National Particle Accelerator Institute. The experiment will begin at 11 AM on June fifteenth. I understand you are the top Stars practitioner of lunar magic and believe you can handle any parasite that may appear. That said, I'm happy to deploy the Team 11 as a precaution."

In the USNA military, mental interference magic was referred to as lunar magic. Though he lacked practical experience, Arcturus was a formidable practitioner. He came from a powerful line of North American indigenous peoples. Since his grandmother was a pure-blooded indigenous shaman, many believed his prowess in mental interference magic came from her.

As a result, Arcturus was excluded from missions involving ancient magic users known as "sorcerers" or "witch doctors" who specialized in mental attack magic. This was discrimination, of course, but there was little he could do.

Caucasians and Asian Americans used the term *sorcerer* to specifically refer to ancient magic users from indigenous communities and *witch doctors* to refer to ancient magic users of African descent. Arcturus had long been subjected to racial prejudice under the suspicion that he might empathize with ethnic-specific ancient magic users.

While all three members of Team 11 also excelled in lunar magic, they didn't suffer from the consequences of prejudice. They were accustomed to dealing with attacks that corroded the mind and were often deployed to confront ancient magic users who specialized in mental interference magic.

"All due respect, sir, I don't need Team 11," Arcturus replied. "My junior officers are more than capable."

He was well aware of his lack of combat experience, but he had a strong sense of pride. He was also convinced that there should be as few people involved in the experiment as possible. Luckily, Walker shared that mindset.

"Suit yourself," Walker said.

Arcturus thought this meant that his Team 3 would be the only ones deployed to the scene. Alas, he was wrong.

"Then I'll have Team 6 on standby outside the research facility," Walker added. "Have them notify me immediately if they spot any suspicious activity."

The three stellar-level members of Team 6, Rigel, Bellatrix, and Alnilam, had all received codenames coinciding with stars in the Orion constellation. Collectively, they were known as the Orion Team. This name was not a coincidence. Team 6 was specifically assembled as a team of hunters skilled in tracking.

"All right," Arcturus conceded. "But if I may—"

"Don't worry," Walker interrupted. "I won't tell them about the experiment."

A look of relief passed briefly over Arcturus's face. The purpose of the micro black hole experiment was to flush out Japanese operatives from the military's ranks. Arcturus knew that the cooperation of other teams would guarantee their capture. At the same time, he preferred they were not aware of the experiment, given its dangerous nature.

Fortunately, Walker agreed. Unfortunately, both parties were inadvertently concealing information from each other that they should have shared.

◇ ◇ ◇

The Japanese government announced that a residential area in the Izu Highlands had been attacked with magic. They harshly condemned the strike without identifying the perpetrator and emphasized the only way to counter such incidents in the future would be to enhance the nation's own magic capabilities.

Not only did these statements make the social exclusion of magicians a humanitarian issue, but they also indirectly criticized anti-magic movements. Ultimately, the government suggested that magician exclusion both weakened the national self-defense systems against foreign powers and put citizens' lives in danger.

The fact that the attacker was a magician was withheld from the public. A strict media blackout was imposed to hide the fact that Tatsuya was the target and Minami was a victim. That said, complete secrecy was impossible.

Those who knew Tatsuya's whereabouts at the time of the attack naturally associated him with the incident. Even those who were unaware of the details deduced the truth through keen magic perception.

* * *

Immediately after the government's announcement, Lieutenant Fujibayashi received a private phone call. Although she was on duty, personal calls could still reach her, thanks to official approval to set up a virtual hotline to the Kudou family for emergencies.

"*Hi, Kyouko. It's Minoru,*" said the voice on the other end of the line.

"Oh, hello, Minoru," Fujibayashi replied. "What a surprise."

The hotline in her office supported only voice communication. Since the caller ID always displayed "Kudou Family," Fujibayashi never knew who was calling until she heard their voice. As far as she knew, it could be her grandfather, her uncle, or even her aunt. Minoru, however, was the last person she'd expected to call.

"*Sorry to bother you during work hours,*" he said to her.

"That's all right. I have some time."

This wasn't just a comforting lie. A few minutes earlier, Fujibayashi had been busy preparing materials for the government's public announcement based on Kazama's data. Now that the press conference was over, everyone involved found themselves temporarily without anything to do.

"Why the sudden call?" Fujibayashi asked. "Has there been some sort of emergency?"

She tried hard to conceal her anxiety. It was rare enough to get a call through the hotline, much less from Minoru. He had never been overbearing—at least not in front of Fujibayashi—but he knew she was currently on duty. It was only natural for her to be nervous.

"*No emergency,*" Minoru reassured her. "*I just needed to ask you something. It has to do with the recent government announcement.*"

"All right." Though her heart was racing, she urged Minoru on in her usual steady tone.

"*The long-distance magic targeted Tatsuya, didn't it?*"

"How did you...?"

Fujibayashi couldn't hide her surprise. It wouldn't be surprising if Tatsuya's close friends at First High knew his whereabouts and associated him with the attack on Izu. Fujibayashi wondered if someone like Leonhard Saijou or Mikihiko Yoshida, whom she had met in Kyoto last autumn, had filled Minoru in. She quickly found out she was wrong.

"I sensed strong magic fluctuations in eastern Japan and thought Tatsuya and his family might be involved."

Fujibayashi was speechless. If what Minoru said was true, it meant he had surpassed Tatsuya's Elemental Sight.

Elemental Sight could see anything as long as it had access to the necessary data. It also required intentionality and direction of will. If Tatsuya didn't actively want to see something or didn't direct his will toward it, he could not see it.

He could only passively sense hostility directed at Miyuki because he narrowed his focus on the target in a way that allowed him to do so. This time, however, he had not actually perceived the attack until it was already on its way.

If Minoru had sensed Tuman Bomba's activation, that meant he had randomly perceived magic occurring nearly four hundred kilometers away. It was possible that Tuman Bomba's potency helped Minoru home in on it. But in Fujibayashi's eyes, his observation proved that his abilities far surpassed Tatsuya's.

Has he gained the power of Elemental Sight? Fujibayashi wondered.

"Since when can you sense magic like this?" she asked.

Unfortunately, Minoru wasn't focused enough to answer her question. His mind was consumed with concern for Tatsuya—or perhaps someone in Tatsuya's party.

"Is Tatsuya safe?" he blurted out. *"Were Miyuki and Sakurai affected?"*

"Tatsuya and Miyuki are fine. Sakurai, on the other hand..."

With her question still unanswered, she found herself caught off guard and unable to deceive Minoru.

"What happened to her?"

The anxiety in his voice forced Fujibayashi to relent.

"She was hospitalized. Dr. Yamanaka suspects she might be suffering from mental strain due to an overuse of magic."

"I thought the Independent Magic Battalion was at the scene when it happened. Didn't they provide any treatment?"

How does he know all this? Fujibayashi thought, bewildered.

There was no way Minoru could have known that the Independent Magic Battalion was at the scene of the attack that morning. The government had not reported anything about the Independent Magic Battalion's whereabouts at the time of the attack. Moreover, only Saeki, Kazama, the other soldiers on duty, and the Yotsuba family were aware of the battalion's deployment.

To make things more confusing, Minoru's words didn't sound like casual speculation. His statement was not only accurate; it was confident. The Minoru that Fujibayashi knew shouldn't be capable of this level of insight. He had always been a talented magician, but he had never shown the ability to discern top secret information.

It's almost like he has been possessed by a demon of forbidden knowledge, Fujibayashi wondered to the point of superstition.

If she hadn't dismissed her own intuition as a mere delusion at that moment, the future might have been very different.

◇ ◇ ◇

Even after his phone call with Fujibayashi, Minoru didn't harbor any feelings of resentment toward the military. He was somewhat disappointed, but he resigned himself to the reality that the National Defense Forces' callousness was common knowledge.

Above all else, he was worried about Minami. Suffering mental damage due to magic overuse usually involved the overheating of the magic-calculation region. This was a unique condition among magicians for which there was currently no treatment.

Magicians who had undergone genetic modifications were especially susceptible to this condition. According to the knowledge

Minoru had absorbed from Gongjin Zhou, a magic-calculation region overload—which was the cause of Minoru's own unstable constitution—had to be the main issue.

In Minoru's case, the limiters that suppressed his magic to tolerable levels failed to function properly. Even for regular magicians, an excessive use of magic in combat could cause the magic-calculation region to exceed the tolerable threshold and force their limiters to break down. Knowledge about the technology to repair this condition was something even Gongjin Zhou didn't have.

I can't cure Minami, but the Yotsuba family might, Minoru thought.

This was more of a wish than anything else, but it was the only way to calm his impatience.

I should go visit her. Seeing her in person should help me stop worrying.

He couldn't imagine Tatsuya would let his own family member die without a fight. Minami was surely receiving the treatment she needed. All Minoru had to do was go see for himself.

He decided to take off from school the next day. While he knew he should limit his absences to sick days, he was also smart enough to make up for poor attendance with his work on exams and reports.

◇ ◇ ◇

Minami was far from comfortable when she awoke. Her body felt heavy, and a profound sense of fatigue permeated her entire being.

When she opened her eyes, she was greeted by a gentle cream-colored ceiling. She turned her head to find the walls were the same color. Her bed was fitted with clean white sheets and a blanket. The prick of an IV needle chafed her left arm.

Is this a hospital? she wondered.

Suddenly, everything came rushing back.

Wait! Where is Miyuki?!

She tried to sit up, only to realize her body was too weak. Even putting all her strength into her movements led to disappointing results.

"Ugh…" She groaned in frustration.

As she lay on her back, trying to regain control of her breathing, there was a knock at the door.

"…Come in," she said quietly.

The weakness of her voice surprised even herself.

"Hi, Minami."

Miyuki!

Even though her mind was still shrouded in a faint haze, Minami had no trouble recognizing that voice. She quickly tried to sit up again, but the results were the same. The best she could do was lift her head a few centimeters. Sadly, it fell back onto her pillow before long. She groaned.

"Minami!" Miyuki exclaimed, running to her side.

Minami turned her head to see Miyuki's face filled with worry. Despite her anxious expression, Miyuki was breathtakingly beautiful. Minami's chest filled with admiration.

She's so pretty, she sighed to herself.

"Don't push yourself too hard," another voice said, snapping Minami out of her daydream.

"Tatsuya…" She gasped. "I'm so glad you two are safe…"

The first thing that came out of her mouth was completely devoted to Tatsuya and Miyuki's well-being.

"It's all thanks to you," Tatsuya said.

"That's kind of you to say," Minami whispered.

Her eyes filled with tears of relief that her efforts had paid off and were fully acknowledged.

"Oh, don't get up," Miyuki said, stopping Minami from trying to move.

"You can talk to us the way you are," Tatsuya added.

Minami finally ceased trying to prop herself up. "I'm sorry," she murmured.

Miyuki was taken aback by this unexpected apology and didn't know what to say. Even Tatsuya fell silent for a moment.

"What are you apologizing for?" he said. "Miyuki and I are only here because of you. That's the truth."

"But I ran out of strength midway," Minami insisted weakly. "A Guardian's job is only complete when she protects her charge. In that sense, I failed."

Her voice was barely audible, and her body was still too feeble to sit upright. Yet there was a spark in her eyes that reflected the strength of her heart.

"Minami, I know you're exhausted, so I don't want to argue with you," Tatsuya told her. "But I will say two things I need you to hear."

"I'm listening," Minami replied.

Tatsuya sat on a stool near Minami's pillow to meet her at eye level and avoid coming off as condescending.

"I admire your sense of duty. I really do," he began. "But I also need you to understand that you just used your magic to block a Tuman Bomba attack. Give yourself some credit."

"…All right," Minami said vaguely.

It was clear she couldn't completely accept Tatsuya's words.

"That's the first thing. Now, here's the second," he continued solemnly.

Both girls drew in a breath at the intensity of his tone, preparing themselves for what might come next.

"I don't only see you as Miyuki's Guardian," he said.

"……"

Minami stared at him in silence.

Her gaze seemed to tacitly ask him, *Then what do you want from me? What do you expect me to be?*

Tatsuya continued.

"There aren't many people in this world who I can depend on. I trust Leo, Erika, Mizuki, and all our friends at First High, but I don't want them getting involved in our private matters. The Yotsuba clan is on our side for now, but I know they would immediately abandon me if I ever got in the way. I have faith in Fumiya and Ayako, but they both have their own roles to play. It's possible I won't be able to count on them when push comes to shove. As for Master Yakumo and Colonel Kazama, there's a decent chance that they may become my enemies one day."

What about me? Minami seemed to ask with her eyes.

"You, on the other hand, I can both trust and depend on," Tatsuya said. "You're one of the few in this entire world. That's why I paired you with Miyuki. I don't want you to be her Guardian; I want you to be her companion."

"Her companion?" Minami echoed weakly.

"I won't force you to do anything you don't want to," Tatsuya explained. "Still, it's my hope that you will be by Miyuki's side for as long as possible, not rushing to your death as her Guardian. At least until you find someone else to spend your life with."

Minami's pale cheeks suddenly flushed. Tatsuya's last comment took her by surprise. Not in her wildest dreams did she imagine he would prioritize her wishes for potential marriage.

"Minami," Miyuki chimed in from her seat beside Tatsuya. "I am so happy you are with me and never want you to throw your life away."

Minami's eyes filled with tears again. She had never felt so loved by Tatsuya and Miyuki.

"Please just rest for now," Miyuki continued. "I think that's what you need most right now."

"All right," Minami replied. "I will try to heal up as fast as possible. Once I'm better, would it be all right if I served you again?"

"Of course," Miyuki replied with a smile. "I would love that."

The door opened behind Tatsuya as a doctor and nurse entered the room.

"We'll come back to visit you tomorrow," Tatsuya said, standing up from his stool.

"See you later, Minami," Miyuki said warmly, standing up as well.

"Thank you for coming," Minami told them.

Tatsuya and Miyuki stepped out of the doctor's way and left the room.

◇ ◇ ◇

After paying Minami a visit, Tatsuya and Miyuki returned to the apartment in Chofu. Tatsuya plopped himself down on the living room sofa as if he had no intention of leaving the house for the rest of the day.

"Will you be staying the night?" Miyuki asked, placing a cup of coffee in front of her brother.

Before Minami had joined them, Miyuki had been the one who served Tatsuya his coffee. While Minami never intended to take over, she simply ended up serving drinks before Miyuki had the chance.

Each time this happened, Miyuki experienced a twinge of guilt. Yet now that Minami was gone, she couldn't help but feel overwhelmed with loneliness. This feeling wasn't unique to Miyuki; it was simply human nature.

"I'm actually planning to leave the Izu villa," Tatsuya said. "If possible, I'd like to go pick up my things as early as tomorrow."

"Then will you be returning for good?" Miyuki asked cautiously, a spark of happiness flitting through her eyes.

She probably would have even been happier about the situation if Minami wasn't in the hospital.

"Returning? I guess you could say that," Tatsuya replied.

Though he had stayed at the Chofu residence several times, he had never lived there. To say he was returning felt strange until he thought of it another way. He wasn't returning to the Chofu residence but to Miyuki's side. If Miyuki was living in this apartment, it seemed only natural to go there and be with her.

"Wonderful," Miyuki said. "I will prepare a room for you right away."

"You don't have to do that. Why don't you take a breather?"

Tatsuya had a feeling Miyuki was even more shocked than he was over Minami's hospitalization. A typical way to deal with these feelings would be to keep busy to distract herself from her anxiety.

But rest was important, too. The home automation system could easily handle the simple task of setting up a room. Tatsuya decided Miyuki should put her thoughts aside for now and take a break.

She seemed reluctant at first, but obediently settled herself on the sofa opposite her brother. After a few minutes of looking uncomfortable, she met his gaze.

"What's wrong?" he said. "Do you have something you want to say?"

"...What are you planning to do with Minami?" Miyuki asked.

"What do you mean?" Tatsuya furrowed his brow. "I have no intention of doing anything she doesn't agree to."

"I'm sorry! I was not implying that at all."

"Oh..." Tatsuya came to a sudden realization. "Do you mean what kind of role I expect her to fill?"

"Well, that, too, but..." Miyuki hesitated.

As she struggled to find the right words, Tatsuya finally understood. It had taken him so long because he himself found it hard to vocalize his feelings. He paused for a moment before speaking.

"I don't want to put her in a situation like this ever again."

As soon as he said this, his hesitation melted away.

"Does that mean you want her to stop being my Guardian?" Miyuki asked.

"Yes." Tatsuya nodded. "It will take a while for the damage to her magic-calculation region to heal. We don't even know if it will ever heal completely. The magic-calculation region is basically a black box, even for magicians like us. We know too little about its structure and properties."

"That is true," Miyuki agreed. "The head of the Ichijou family is on the mend, but there's no guarantee that Minami will be as fortunate."

"Right. Even the former head of the Juumonji family lost his magic after intentionally overloading his magic-calculation region. We shouldn't be overly optimistic when it comes to treatment."

Both their faces clouded with concern.

"Besides," Tatsuya added solemnly, "even if Minami recovers this time, there's no guarantee her magic-calculation region won't overheat again."

"As long as she uses magic, you mean?"

"Yeah. And next time, performing first aid might not be enough to save her."

An anxious shadow progressed even farther across Miyuki's face.

"Does that mean Minami can no longer be a magician?" she asked.

"Not exactly. She can still live as a normal magician..."

"...As long as she doesn't participate in intense battles."

"Right. In other words, it's impossible for her to continue as a Guardian where retreat isn't an option. Avoiding combat is key."

"Do you think Minami will be all right with that?"

"Fighting is not the only way to live. I'd like her to have a more peaceful life."

Miyuki's complexion brightened slightly, but worry still lingered on her face. "What about...? Actually, never mind."

What about you? Don't you have the right to live a peaceful life, too?

These questions lingered on the tip of Miyuki's tongue, but she stopped herself from voicing them.

She realized there was no point in asking such things. Even if Tatsuya wanted a more peaceful life, his situation wouldn't allow it. His ability to use strategic magic alone, regardless of whether he used it or not, made him a target for enemies and allies alike.

"Okay," Tatsuya said.

He knew what Miyuki had wanted to say, possibly even better than she knew herself. All the more reason to simply let it go.

[3]

It was Monday, June 10. Though Miyuki, Tatsuya, and Minami had been subjected to a long-range magic attack just the day before, everyday life relentlessly continued. Miyuki attended First High as usual with Minami's condition weighing on her mind.

Tatsuya, on the other hand, had time to keep Minami company in the hospital. Still unable to support her body independently, she wore a power-assist device called an exoskeleton attached to her upper body.

"You must be very busy," she said apologetically, sitting up on her reclining bed.

"I'm still on break from school." Tatsuya shrugged. "Don't worry about me."

"But…" Minami faltered.

She couldn't help but worry, and Tatsuya knew it. He forcibly changed the subject to avoid any impractical questions. There was also a part of him that was curious about the exoskeleton she was wearing.

"Anyway," Tatsuya said, "wouldn't it be better for you to lie down than prop yourself up like that?"

"The doctor said it's better to sit regularly, even if it involves support. He said it would help me return to daily life more quickly."

"Well, that doesn't look very comfortable."

He recognized the power-assist function in the exoskeleton as the same one in his Moval suit. Its response time was fast enough not to interfere with its user's movement. Of course, since medical equipment could not compare with cutting-edge military gear, there were going to be differences in performance. But at the very least, Minami shouldn't have to worry about any inconveniences.

The exoskeleton also supported its own weight, so the wearer didn't feel burdened. However, because it had to be securely fixed to the body, it inevitably felt constricting. Tatsuya doubted it was comfortable at all, but Minami strangely didn't seem to mind.

"It's all right," she said. "The sensation in my limbs hasn't fully returned yet, so I don't really notice it."

Tatsuya was visibly surprised by her answer. "Sensation loss…?" Tatsuya asked when he came back to his senses, keeping his voice low.

His earnest tone made Minami feel a bit flustered, especially because she wasn't too concerned with the abnormalities happening in her own body.

"I wouldn't go that far," she replied quickly. "My senses just feel a little numb."

"What did the doctor say about that?"

"I was told there was no sign of damage to my brain or nerve tissues, so he thinks it is just a temporary anomaly due to exhaustion."

"I hope he's right." Tatsuya spoke calmly, but his face remained tinged with worry.

"Tatsuya, may I ask you a question?" Minami said rather abruptly.

In retrospect, even she didn't know why she said this. The only explanation was that she couldn't hold back the curiosity lingering in her mind.

"Go ahead," said Tatsuya.

"Why do you worry about me so much?"

At first, Tatsuya frowned, as if not understanding the question. But realization quickly crossed his face, paired with a wry smile on his lips.

"I can see how it's strange for someone as emotionless as me to be concerned with a stranger's well-being."

"Th-that's not what I meant!" Minami said quickly.

"Don't worry about it." Tatsuya shrugged. "You're not wrong."

Minami suddenly realized that, sure enough, her question took for granted that Tatsuya was emotionless. She was so ashamed about this that she couldn't even muster up an excuse.

"The only issue I have is that you assume I see you as a stranger," Tatsuya added.

"What?" She gasped.

Her reaction could be interpreted in multiple ways. Luckily, Tatsuya didn't take it poorly.

"How much do you really know about me?" he asked.

Given Minami's position, this was a difficult question to answer. Tatsuya knew this, so he continued without waiting too long.

"It's true I don't express many emotions unless Miyuki is involved. You could even say I lack strong emotions altogether."

Minami knew this much, so she kept silent. Everything Tatsuya was saying was much too big a secret to tell a stranger.

"To tell you the truth, Miyuki thinks of you like a sister," Tatsuya continued. "And your bond helps me feel close to you, too. I worry about you because Miyuki worries about you from the bottom of her heart. This might seem superficial, but my earnest concern for you comes through her."

"That actually…means a lot," Minami said. "I'm honored."

It meant the world to her that Miyuki thought of her like a sister. She was also flattered that Tatsuya included her in his affections for Miyuki. Something told her that Tatsuya was being genuine when he said this.

"You're…honored?" Tatsuya asked, confused.

"No, it's nothing. Please don't worry about it.".

Uncertain that she could explain it well in words, she decided to drop the subject. Tatsuya seemed fine with this choice.

"I'll stop by later tonight with Miyuki," he said. "In the meantime, forget about work and focus on getting better."

"Of course." Minami bowed her head as much as she could.

◇ ◇ ◇

Initially, Miyuki wanted to skip school on this day. She wasn't confident that she could focus on class with her head full of worry. More than anything, she wanted nothing more than to stay by Minami's side.

At the same time, she knew her presence wouldn't help Minami heal. In fact, being near Minami for long periods of time could even stimulate her magic-calculation region with psion waves and block the healing process. At least that's what the doctors said, so Miyuki decided to play it safe.

She didn't mean to send psion waves flying all over the place. When Oath consumed her control over her magic, she simply couldn't help it. Now that she had regained control, she felt guilty that her magic still caused trouble for others.

Compared to Tatsuya, who had complete control over his psions, Miyuki had to admit that her control was still lacking. Though not as much as Tatsuya, she possessed a significantly higher amount of psions than the average magician, and it was very possible that this psion influx had a negative impact on Minami's health. That was why she decided against staying at the hospital and went to First High instead.

As soon as Miyuki entered the classroom, Honoka and Shizuku approached her with concerned looks.

"Are you okay, Miyuki?" Shizuku asked.

"What do you mean?"

Miyuki wasn't trying to play dumb. The question simply caught her off guard. If her situation needed to be kept a secret, she would have to be careful about recklessly spreading information. But in this case, caution was unnecessary.

"Wasn't the location of the attack the government announced yesterday the same area where Tatsuya's villa is?" Honoka said. "You told us you were sleeping over, remember?"

Clearly, Honoka and Shizuku had connected the dots well enough to figure out that Tatsuya had been the target of the long-distance magic attack.

"Oh, yes...," Miyuki began, taking a seat. "Tatsuya and I are fine, but Minami is in the hospital."

"No!" Honoka gasped.

"Was she injured?" Shizuku asked.

Since her desk was in the front of the row, she spun back in her chair to face Miyuki.

"Not physically injured," Miyuki said hesitantly, "but something like that."

Overheating of the magic-calculation region was not yet considered a common condition among magicians. Though it was mental rather than physical, it was still fair to classify it as an injury.

Rather than pressing the issue further, Shizuku simply said, "I see. Is it bad?"

"Well, we are not sure when she will be discharged," Miyuki replied sadly.

Shizuku and Honoka looked concerned.

"That's awful," Shizuku said.

"Could we go visit her?" Honoka asked.

"...She's not contagious, so that should be fine," Miyuki replied slowly. "But I will check with her doctor, just to be safe."

While she was happy that her friends cared about Minami, the situation wasn't exactly one that welcomed crowds. It was important to exercise caution.

"Okay," Shizuku said.

"Let us know if you get the doctor's approval," Honoka added, kneeling at Miyuki's desk.

"I will." Miyuki nodded with a faint smile.

◇ ◇ ◇

At a little past 11 AM, there was a knock at Minami's hospital room door.

"Who is it?" she called curiously.

She knew Tatsuya was in Izu, and Miyuki should have been at school. While the hospital was sponsored by the Yotsuba family, it wasn't limited to Yotsuba members. In fact, it was a general hospital open to the public.

Minami was informed the block she was in was strictly monitored, so she wasn't worried about dangerous people sneaking around. She simply thought the knock at her door was a visitor to a Yotsuba family patient who had gotten the rooms mixed up.

"It's Minoru Kudou," a voice on the other side of the door replied.

This was the last person Minami could have expected.

"M-Minoru?!" she yelped.

What she meant to say was something like, *"Why are you here?"* or *"How did you know I was in the hospital?"* But the shock of his sudden visit made her draw a complete blank. Luckily, her surprise lasted only a moment before she became acutely aware of how she must have looked.

She'd made herself presentable when Tatsuya visited that morning, but she had been napping since then. Her hair, especially, was probably a mess. She couldn't stand Minoru seeing her like this.

"J-just a minute!" she called.

She hastily forced her sluggish right hand toward a large button on the wired controller attached to the inside of her bed. The upper half of the bed rose, lifting her body and moving the exoskeleton to fit onto both of her sides so that she was leaning lightly against the backrest.

Now that the bed was raised, a gap formed between the mattress and Minami's spine. The right and the left parts of the exoskeleton connected through this gap and secured themselves to her upper body.

Using the support from the portion of the exoskeleton around her arms, Minami picked up a hand mirror and hairbrush and quickly tidied her disheveled hair. She wished she could apply some makeup, but she lacked the tools. Besides, fixing her hair was physically all she could manage at this point.

"A-all right. You can come in now," Minami announced.

Her room's AI recognized this as a command and unlocked the door.

"Hello?" Minoru said hesitantly as he walked in.

Suddenly, the room filled with what seemed to be a holy light.

Minoru was like a celestial being descending from the heavens, the sole hint of color in the pristine white hospital room. At least that was how Minami saw him.

"Um, how are you doing, Sakurai?" Minoru asked with a shy smile.

He didn't notice the strange look Minami was giving him. Or perhaps he was so used to receiving these kinds of looks that it didn't bother him. Thanks to Minoru's regular tone, Minami quickly snapped back to reality. Regaining her senses, a series of questions began to take shape in her mind.

How did Minoru know I was hospitalized? And who told him I was in this hospital?

But instead of raising these questions, she simply answered Minoru's.

"I'm not in pain. My body is still weak, but the doctors said it will heal in time."

"That's good to hear," Minoru replied with a smile.

Minami's pale cheeks flushed pink. If Minoru's smile had lasted a second longer, Minami might have fainted from something other than fatigue. As the boy stared at her solemnly, Minami didn't even realize that her consciousness was gradually fading. She wondered why he wasn't at school, but even this question vanished from her mind.

"Is there anything else?" Minoru asked in a doctor-like manner.

"Wh-what do you mean?" Minami stammered, snapping back to reality.

"Do you have foggy vision or muffled hearing?"

"......"

Minami hesitated to tell Minoru about the dulling of her senses, afraid it would cause him unnecessary worry. Eventually, Minoru's sincere gaze dispelled her caution to the wind.

"I know you think telling me about this won't make much difference, but this is important," he said. "So please, answer honestly!"

"My sense of touch is a little—"

"—So you're experiencing a loss of sensation!" Minoru gasped, drawing closer to her. "Is that right, Sakurai?"

Unable to bear how close his face was, Minami averted her gaze. Needless to say, her behavior had nothing to do with disgust. It was more about an inability to maintain eye contact than a gesture of embarrassment.

"Y-yes," she managed. "And as I said before, you can call me Minami."

Her sudden request took Minoru off guard. He pulled away from her at a speed that could be called anything but subtle.

Once he was at a distance Minami could tolerate, he stammered, "B-but..."

Despite his good looks, Minoru had zero experience with romantic relationships. His captivating beauty and mysterious aura had always made girls hesitate to approach him. Though he was in no way a social pariah, he wasn't exactly charismatic, either, and he found it challenging to address a cute girl by her first name.

Many boys felt their inhibitions unexpectedly go numb around

an exceptionally stunning girl like Miyuki. Minami, on the other hand, who Minoru saw as the girl-next-door type, was just adorable enough to make him bashful.

"If you don't call me by my first name, I'll have to start calling you Kudou," Minami murmured, glancing away with tears in her eyes.

Given their respective social positions, Minami was expected to address Minoru by his last name. The only reason she didn't was to maintain the balance between how he addressed Tatsuya and Miyuki. Since calling them both "Shiba" would get confusing, Minoru called them by their first names. It only made sense they return the favor. That said, whenever Tatsuya and Miyuki weren't present, it was still more appropriate for Minami to address Minoru by his last name. She knew this, of course, but she didn't like the idea of losing the small privilege.

Her dejected expression made Minoru forget his bashfulness for a moment. Besides, he didn't like the idea of Minami addressing him so formally.

"All right. Minami, then," he said almost automatically.

"Good." Minami nodded. "And you can remain Minoru."

"……"

"……"

Of course, the bashfulness between the two had not completely disappeared. Their combined embarrassment filled the hospital room with a youthful tension.

"Um, anyway…" Minoru dithered. "What did the doctor say about your loss of sensation?"

"Oh, um… He said they didn't see any brain or nerve damage, so it's probably just temporary," Minami replied.

Her companion's sudden frown made the bundle of suppressed anxiety swell within Minami's chest. Despite her attempts to act nonchalant about the strange changes in her body, she was terrified deep down.

The Yotsuba family had taught her how unstable the life of an engineered magician could be, and she knew she could share their fate someday. In fact, she had a feeling the time to face that reality may have already come.

She would have been less worried if all she felt was fatigue. It was the obvious abnormality in her physical sensations that proved concerning. She knew the cause lay in the overload of her magic-calculation region. She was also aware of the close ties between engineered magicians' overuse of magic and their sudden deaths.

Minami pushed her magic to the limit to protect Miyuki. She was always ready to risk her life for her and still had no regrets. These past few days she had tried not to dwell on the real consequences of her actions, putting on a brave front and deceiving herself. But now that Minoru stood before her with a grim look on his face, the anxiety she had been avoiding all this time suddenly weighed heavily upon her.

"Do you mind if I touch your hand?" Minoru asked Minami.

"Oh, sure."

Though calm didn't come naturally in front of Minoru, the anxiety spreading within her helped dull her shyness.

She extended her right hand with the exoskeleton's support. Surprisingly, it was Minoru who felt more embarrassed now, despite having initiated the gesture. His fair cheeks flushed slightly as he gently held Minami's hand between his two palms.

Minami couldn't help but blush, too. Minoru slowly moved his right hand, his cheeks still red but his expression serious. Minami found herself drawn into the boy's intensely warm gaze. She suspected that his occasional frown indicated he was sensing something unknown, something even the doctors and Minami herself couldn't understand.

After about a minute, Minoru released Minami's hand and sighed. It was as if he had been so focused, he had forgotten to breathe. Minami also let out a subtle sigh, but hers was out of nervousness. Minoru didn't even notice.

"Minami, this might be hard to hear, but your injuries have not completely healed," he said. "Your magic-calculation region is still heavily damaged. You may be feeling okay now, but you could collapse at any moment."

"Oh."

"I know it's hard to believe."

On the contrary, Minami had a feeling this was true all along. Minoru's comment simply helped her acknowledge something she had sensed deep down.

"That said, I need you to trust me," Minoru continued.

Minami looked up at Minoru in surprise, unsure what he meant.

"I'll find a cure for you," he told her, "so please don't give up."

Why does he care about me so much? Minami thought.

She had posed the same question to Tatsuya that morning, but for some reason, it felt harder to ask now.

"All right," she said. "Thank you, Minoru."

Her kind words came as a surprise to them both.

◇ ◇ ◇

Meanwhile, Tatsuya was busy clearing out the villa in Izu. While he had help with packing his bags and loading them onto a truck, he couldn't entrust the transfer of his research data to anyone else.

At around 1 PM, he took a break for lunch. Since the kitchen utensils belonged to the villa, Pixie prepared Tatsuya's meal as usual. It wasn't just the kitchen utensils. Most of the villa items, even his clothes, had been provided for him by the Yotsuba family. This left little for Tatsuya to pack and take back to the Chofu apartment. The only reason he was eating lunch this late was because he had become so involved in his work.

Tatsuya sat alone at the dining room table while the movers snacked on boxed lunches in their trucks. Not wanting to make them uncomfortable, Tatsuya didn't insist on eating all together.

After Pixie had cleared his plate and served him a cup of coffee,

Hyougo Hanabishi entered the room. Rather than his usual three-piece suit, he was dressed in work pants and a jacket resembling a delivery company's uniform. Since he was so young, the casual attire suited him. Or at least he didn't look out of place. His usual polite bow, on the other hand, exuded indescribable discomfort.

"Apologies for interrupting your lunch," Hyougo said to Tatsuya.

"It's all right. I just finished. Did you want to talk to me about something?"

"I received news from the doctors at Chofu Aoba Hospital."

Chofu Aoba Hospital was where Minami was hospitalized. For a minute, Tatsuya panicked that Minami's condition had taken a turn for the worse, but he quickly regained his calm. If anything had happened to her, Hyougo would sound a lot tenser.

"What is it?" Tatsuya asked him.

"Sakurai had a visitor at a little past eleven this morning."

As a Yotsuba family butler, Hyougo was of a higher rank than Minami, who he considered a mere maid. This meant he felt comfortable enough to call her by her last name without any titles or embellishments.

"A visitor?" Tatsuya repeated suspiciously. "I was told there would be strict limits on that."

"There are, but the hospital staff insists they couldn't turn this visitor away," Hyougo explained. "Apparently, even the Yotsuba family ultimately granted him permission to enter."

"So who was this visitor?"

It clearly wasn't a random person if the hospital staff felt they couldn't turn him away. The fact that Maya had given her approval made the situation even more cryptic. Tatsuya had no idea who the visitor could be.

"The third son of the Kudou clan, Minoru Kudou," Hyougo replied.

Minoru was the youngest in his family with two older sisters and two older brothers.

"Minoru?" Tatsuya repeated.

The first thought that came to his mind was an obvious one: *Why was Minoru at the hospital on a school day?*

He didn't question how Minoru knew Minami was hospitalized. Fujibayashi must have told him. Though Minami's hospitalization should have been classified information, Fujibayashi had a soft spot for her little brother. If he went to her asking about Minami, she would have told him what he wanted to know. The location of Minami's hospital wasn't important enough to the National Defense Force for Fujibayashi to keep it a secret.

What confused Tatsuya the most was why Minoru would go to the trouble of skipping school to visit Minami. The two had only been around each other for less than three days in the past. They seemed to get along well enough, but there were no signs of any special affection between them.

It was possible Minoru developed feelings for Minami when she nursed him back to health in Kyoto, but Tatsuya found this too convenient. To be fair, he didn't know Minoru that well. Still. Recklessly skipping school and traveling all the way from Nara to Tokyo to visit a girl felt out of character for the boy, at least from Tatsuya's perspective.

"Is he still at the hospital now?" he asked.

He considered going there directly to question Minoru himself. Unfortunately, these plans were foiled.

"No, he already left," Hyougo said. "He was only there for about twenty minutes."

Tatsuya was surprised at how quickly Minoru moved. He wasn't sure if twenty minutes was long or short compared to the typical hospital visit, but it did seem abrupt, especially since Minoru took the day off from school.

Did his visit have an ulterior motive? Tatsuya wondered. He didn't have enough information to make conjectures, so he put that aside.

"All right. That's enough about Minoru. Is there anything else?" Tatsuya asked.

"No, that is all," Hyougo replied with an elegant bow before leaving the room.

Once he was alone, Tatsuya turned to Pixie, who had become stiff as a statue in the corner of the dining room.

"Pixie, bring me my information terminal," he ordered.

"*Yes, Master*," she answered through her mechanical speakers and obediently did as she was told.

Tatsuya had exchanged contact information with Minoru the previous autumn. They had not spoken to each other since the Gongjin Zhou incident, but Tatsuya figured Minoru's ID should still be the same.

Communication IDs attached to information terminals were designed to prevent reuse, so the former one was void once changed to something new. The fact that Tatsuya heard a ringing tone meant Minoru's ID should still be valid.

If Minoru had changed his ID, Tatsuya would have received an automated message saying he had called an invalid ID. He would have received a similar message if Minoru's terminal was off. So either Minoru's information terminal was out of reach, or he was intentionally avoiding Tatsuya's call.

This isn't like him, Tatsuya thought.

Then again, he didn't know Minoru well enough to draw any substantial conclusions. He decided to temporarily set his doubts aside and wait.

◇ ◇ ◇

When Tatsuya called, Minoru was already on the long-distance trailer train heading for Nara. However, this was no excuse for why he didn't answer the call. Trailers were essentially trains made up of cabinet compartments. Passengers usually transferred to the main part of the trailer to stretch their legs, but they could also remain in their respective compartment. Minoru chose to do the latter.

Each compartment was a fully private space. Even if Minoru had answered Tatsuya's call, he wouldn't disturb anyone. The only reason he didn't answer was because he didn't hear his terminal ring. At that moment, he was engrossed in an internal conversation. Not with himself but with the ghost of Gongjin Zhou, which he had absorbed through exotype magic. The intense focus it took to maintain this conversation made him miss Tatsuya's call.

Minoru asked the ghost about a way to cure Minami. The answer was discouraging, to say the least.

It will be very difficult to heal the girl's magic-calculation region, Gongjin's ghost said.

Then a cure is impossible? Minoru asked. *But why? The head of the Ichijou clan was in a similar situation and is doing just fine.*

While Gouki Ichijou's collapse was shrouded in mystery, many members of the Ten Master Clans believed it was a result of the overheating of his magic-calculation region. The Ichijou family had recently announced their clan head's smooth recovery, which the Kudou family had confirmed with their own eyes.

The damage Gouki Ichijou suffered was not that serious, the ghost replied.

Then will Minami be in her current state forever?! Minoru demanded.

She may heal physically, the ghost explained. *The doctors were not lying about that.*

What do you mean?

As long as she has enough bed rest, her physical weakness and dulled senses should quickly return to normal.

This gave Minoru some peace of mind, but only for an instant.

If damage to her magic-calculation region caused her current physical situation, shouldn't we do something to prevent any repercussions? he asked.

The likelihood of a natural repercussion is low, the ghost replied. *Unlike "us," her body is not constantly activating excessive psions to cause physical strain.*

Gongjin's composed observation grated on Minoru's nerves. Generally speaking, a high level of psion activity in a magician's body was a mark of great talent. In Minoru's case, however, the same psion activity had become the very shackles that bound him to his bed.

But this was not the time to be frustrated with his own situation. He couldn't afford to be consumed by his own helplessness. Right now, his priority was to find treatment for Minami.

Are you saying an increase in psion activity could cause physical repercussions? he asked.

Psions activated in a magician's body whenever they used magic. The stronger the magic, the higher the psion activity. If an increase in psion activity proved harmful, that meant Minami would collapse every time she used a high-level spell in the future. In other words, she would completely lose the ability to cast advanced magic.

Correct, the ghost affirmed. *Unlike* us, *the girl's condition is clear, so there shouldn't be any impact on her daily life. However, her activities as a magician will be limited much like* ours *are.*

Minoru gritted his teeth. The inability to perform as a magician was something that had been tormenting him for years. At this point, it was unbearable. He wondered if Minami would feel the same.

Okay, Minoru said slowly, *but she should still be able to live a normal life, right?*

Unfortunately, it's impossible to say for sure, Gongjin replied. *The blood of an engineered magician runs through her veins. Her parents were likely engineered magicians as well. Even if she does not actively use magic herself, there is always a possibility that her magic-calculation region could go haywire and exceed her body's tolerance levels.*

Like me, Minoru thought.

Actually, her situation would be much worse than ours. Our *soul may lack strength, but it possesses high regenerative abilities. That is why* we *manage to survive our many collapses without succumbing to death. In the girl's case, however, a single breakdown of the soul might cause her to lose her life altogether.*

But she survived this time, Minoru noted.

Yes, well...someone must have healed her soul.

Minoru knew right away that it was Tatsuya. He didn't know the full extent of Tatsuya's magic abilities, but he witnessed his classmate's miraculous comeback after a near-fatal attack from Masaki Ichijou during the televised Monolith Code two summers ago. That was enough to prove that Tatsuya was capable of advanced self-healing magic, which he could surely use on others.

Then if the person who saved her isn't around when she collapses..., Minoru began.

She will most likely not survive, Gongjin finished. *Engineered magicians face a life of tragedy. In Minami's case, that tragedy has simply moved closer to home now.*

Could she be cured by the same method that I could? Minoru asked.

Yes. Gongjin agreed. *Becoming one with a parasite would be the most effective way.*

Minoru cut off his connection with Gongjin's ghost. The only way he could save Minami was to turn her into a parasite. But that was impossible. Still, the fact that she had become like him drew him to her even more.

◇ ◇ ◇

As promised, Tatsuya accompanied Miyuki to the hospital that evening. He took the opportunity to ask Minami directly about the purpose for Minoru's visit.

"He said he would find you a cure?" Tatsuya said to her.

"That's right."

It was just as Tatsuya thought. Minoru's purpose for stopping by the hospital went beyond a simple visit. When he heard that the boy had held Minami's hand, he suspected something inappropriate, but he reluctantly accepted that Minoru's true intentions lay in Minami's treatment.

"Does Minoru have the knowledge to find such a cure?" Miyuki asked her brother.

This was a fair question. The Yotsuba clan had long been searching for a cure for magic-calculation region damage without any luck.

"I couldn't say," Tatsuya replied. "During last year's Thesis Competition, he showed that his insights far surpass the average high school student. The former Lab Nine's research, which his family oversaw, also involved many ancient magic techniques related to magic interference. All I can say is it's not entirely impossible that Minoru has learned how to treat the magic-calculation region."

"Magic-calculation region research has been the focus of Yotsuba research since the days of former Lab Four, but they have yet to develop a definitive treatment," Miyuki argued. "Besides, Minoru himself struggles with an imbalance between his magic-calculation region and physical body. If he knew about a treatment for it, wouldn't he prioritize curing himself?"

"Maybe his condition has made him especially knowledgeable about possible cures." Tatsuya shrugged. "Anyway, it's pointless to speculate about that now. If he wants to find treatment for Minami, let's just take him up on his goodwill and move on."

"You're right," Miyuki said. "It was rude of me to doubt him."

Tatsuya turned to Minami.

"The doctors here are working hard on your treatment, too. The Yotsuba family has stepped up their research efforts, and I'm not sitting by idly, either. Let's wait patiently for some good news."

He meant to soothe Minami's anxiety, but it backfired.

"Right," Minami replied hesitantly. "Could I ask you a favor?"

"What is it?" Tatsuya asked, calmly holding back his disappointment at his failed plan.

"If you have a chance, could you tell Minoru not to push himself too hard?"

This took Tatsuya by surprise. Minami's worries clearly lay not in the success of the cure but in Minoru's well-being.

"Did you sense something off about him today?" Tatsuya asked.

"Yes. He seems to be stretching himself too thin, and it's not just because he is worried about me. It is almost as if he is carrying some kind of grave secret."

"He didn't seem ill, did he?"

"No, he looked fine physically."

"I'm worried," Miyuki chimed in, as if Minami's fears had rubbed off on her.

"Minoru is a smart guy. He wouldn't do anything rash," Tatsuya told her.

He wasn't completely sure about this since he wasn't an expert on Minoru's character, but they had been close enough the previous autumn. Tatsuya was pretty sure the boy wouldn't do anything foolish.

Then again, he thought vaguely, *Minoru's behavior today didn't align with my impression of him from the last time we met.*

[4]

First High was a straight shot from the closest cabinet station. There were a few side streets you could take, but it was essentially a single path. Most students went this way to school. The only exceptions were those who lived within walking distance from campus.

The groups of students along the main road to First High were bustling with gossip on the morning of June 11. The famous student council president, Miyuki Shiba, was walking to school with a male student. This particular student was just as famous as she was. In fact, at this point, the scale of his fame was probably even greater. His name was Tatsuya Shiba. For the first time in weeks, he was attending school.

A voice called out as soon as Tatsuya walked through the school gates, and a group of students rushed against the crowd.

"Tatsuya! I can't believe you're back!" Honoka squealed.

Students who were aware of Tatsuya's situation looked on with grace, but those who weren't gave the group strange looks. Honoka couldn't care less as she made her way to Tatsuya's side.

"Thanks," Tatsuya replied. "I look forward to seeing more of you guys from now on."

He wore a slightly wry smile on his lips, but he didn't treat Honoka rudely. As he continued toward school, he spotted someone behind Honoka. It was Shizuku, looking shy as she greeted Tatsuya with a silent glance.

Behind Shizuku was Erika, who rolled her eyes at Honoka's fangirl behavior but gave Tatsuya a casual wave when their eyes met. Leo, Mikihiko, and Mizuki followed. Tatsuya walked into school with Miyuki on his left and Honoka on his right.

The entrance to the Magic Engineering Department was on the junior side of the school. This was because the entrances were divided between Classes A to D and Classes E to H due to the structure of the main school building. After parting ways with Miyuki, Honoka, Shizuku, and Mikihiko, Tatsuya headed to his classroom with Erika, Leo, and Mizuki.

It had been a while since he had visited Class 3-E. Though Erika and Leo were in Class 3-F, they followed him into the Class 3-E classroom.

"My desk is still here," Tatsuya noted as he reached his seat next to the window.

This wasn't sarcasm; he was genuinely surprised. His friends couldn't help but smile behind him. Mizuki took her seat beside Tatsuya and turned to face him.

"Will your stellar reactor project be running without you?" she asked him.

"No, it keeps me busy. I don't even know if I can come to school every day."

Sadness flitted across Mizuki's face, but she quickly hid it with a smile.

"Well, we would love it if you could stop by every now and then," she said.

Erika, who had leaned against the window, nodded in agreement.

"At least walk Miyuki to school," she said. "It gets lonely around here without you."

"You're fine with me just walking Miyuki to school?" Tatsuya scoffed.

He found it funny that Erika was completely disregarding the purpose of school, but it wasn't a bad idea.

"On a different note, how is Sakurai doing?" Leo asked.

He was keenly aware of Minami's absence, since they were in the same club.

"The doctors say she won't have any scars, but it will take time to heal," Tatsuya answered.

"Oh...," Leo murmured.

While Leo was simply concerned about Minami's condition, it was more complicated for Tatsuya. Of course, Tatsuya genuinely hoped for Minami's quick recovery. But at the same time, he had to think about a replacement for Miyuki's protection.

He had let Miyuki go to and from school alone the day before. There weren't many people—magicians and non-magicians alike—who could harm her. Besides, Tatsuya was confident he could protect her even if he wasn't nearby. The issue was that having someone physically with Miyuki at all times would serve as peace of mind.

The Yotsuba family couldn't send just anyone into the school. An older person could pose as a staff member, but it would be impossible to provide a student who was always by Miyuki's side. Tatsuya had already considered escorting his fiancée to and from school himself, even before Erika had suggested it.

◇ ◇ ◇

Tatsuya's return to First High wasn't a sign that the commotion around the Dione Project had settled. In fact, the situation had gotten worse after Tatsuya proposed his own plan. The absence of the media around First High was probably only a result of the attempted shooting. Now that Taurus Silver's identity was public, reporters were hesitant to risk their lives for the sake of an old story.

The main change was that the commotion had expanded to a global scale, away from Tatsuya's immediate surroundings. Among the four great powers, the New Soviet Union was now the only nation supporting the USNA's Dione Project. Although an official government statement had not been released, the Indo-Persian Federation showed support for Tatsuya's ESCAPES Plan, and the Great Asian Alliance had yet to choose sides.

Countries outside the four great powers also held various stances regarding the issue. European nations tended to support the Dione Project, while countries from West to Southeast Asia supported the ESCAPES Plan. Like the Great Asian Alliance, Brazil and Australia remained neutral for the time being.

A lack of overt confrontation from both sides complicated the situation. On the surface, both the Dione Project and the ESCAPES Plan shared a common goal toward the peaceful use of magic. Moreover, neither project officially sought to eliminate the other. As far as the public knew, implementing the Dione Project did not inherently obstruct the progress of the ESCAPES Plan, and vice versa. The only drawback was that magicians couldn't participate in both projects simultaneously.

On the one hand, the ongoing publicity battle between Tatsuya and Edward Clark was currently leaning in Tatsuya's favor. This advantage didn't necessarily point to Tatsuya's intellectual superiority over Clark. Tatsuya was simply at an advantage since he had most recently presented his case.

On the other hand, the two magicians' feud was a continuous, unregulated competition, making victory uncertain. Now that Edward Clark was falling behind, he resorted to a power tactic.

◇ ◇ ◇

During First High's first period of the day, Hiromi Saeki, ranked major general and commanding officer of the National Defense Force's 101st Brigade, paid a visit to the Ministry of Defense. Though the building was known first and foremost as the workplace of the

Joint Chiefs of Staff, Saeki was summoned to the section dedicated to staff officers. She returned to the brigade base's command room before noon and immediately called for Kazama.

"Did you want to talk to me about Tatsuya—I mean, Mr. Tatsuya Shiba?" Kazama began.

"No need to uphold formalities with me, Colonel," Saeki interjected.

It wasn't like her to disrupt the conversation like this. She also wasn't the type to hide her anger. Rather than being shocked by her change of behavior, Kazama found it amusing. He tensed his abdomen to suppress a chuckle as he stood before her desk.

"My apologies," he said. "I heard you were ordered to convince Tatsuya to join the Dione Project."

"The section chief at the Ministry of Foreign Affairs doesn't have the authority to give me orders," Saeki stated plainly.

The section chief of the North American branch's Ministry of Foreign Affairs had met Saeki in a conference room at the Ministry of Defense. As she said, he lacked the authority to issue orders to the National Defense Force. Anything the section chief may have told Saeki was most likely presented as a request. That said, if a defense ministry secretary had been present, all so-called requests would be embedded with de facto coercion. In other words, they were essentially orders.

Military officers generally hated when others disrupted chain of command, and Saeki was no exception. The fact that someone was trying to interfere with her power was at the root of her anger.

"Of course," Kazama conceded. "Were you requested to negotiate with Tatsuya because he is Ryuuya Ooguro?"

"So it seems," Saeki replied coldly.

Kazama let out an audible sigh, unable to hide his frustration. "That means the staff officers are not fully aware of the nature of the position Tatsuya held."

"It's understandable," Saeki said. "The position of Specialist Ooguro is, in a sense, extralegal."

The current National Defense Force did not have a formal system for special officers. In fact, from a historical perspective, it wasn't even entirely appropriate to label Tatsuya as such. It was much more accurate to refer to him as a member of the militia who was granted officer status. Since there wasn't a single term that fit that description, the National Defense Force used "special officer" as a placeholder. Unfortunately, this meant anyone unaware of his situation might think Tatsuya was a regular military officer.

"Especially since they are in charge of legal matters, I believe it's crucial for administration to be informed," Kazama said.

He recognized that Tatsuya's position was extralegal, which allowed the National Defense Force to resolve any issues regarding the position internally. However, since some staff officers were briefed as part of this process, the fact that certain personnel in the Ministry of Defense were not privy to this information could be considered negligence on the National Defense Force's end and possibly punished.

"You're right, of course," Saeki replied. "But we have more pressing matters at the moment."

"Forgive me," Kazama said. "Are you referring to whether we can or even should try to convince Tatsuya to join the Dione Project?"

"Correct."

"All right. Well, do both the Ministry of Defense and Ministry of Foreign Affairs know Tatsuya is the caster of Material Burst?"

"Not as far as I could tell today."

"Interesting," Kazama mused. "I can see why they would give you such inexplicable instructions, then."

Tatsuya was not only Japan's greatest magic asset; he was also its key military weapon. In many ways, he was a wild card—the strongest person capable of single-handedly shifting the global balance. Though he proved troublesome for various reasons, the military world was no stranger to wild cards. Willingly giving him up would be foolish. If the government truly understood that Tatsuya was currently the most powerful strategic-class magician in the world, they wouldn't even consider involving him in the Dione Project.

"Why not just name Tatsuya as the fourteenth Apostle?" Kazama suggested on a whim.

Saeki looked surprised, but this lasted only a moment.

"That's not a bad idea," she replied.

"Ma'am?"

Now Kazama was surprised. He had only meant what he said as a joke.

"It may be worth considering that option if the situation continues to worsen," Saeki explained. "Once it becomes clear that Tatsuya is a strategic magician, the government will be much less likely to hand him over to the USNA."

"That's true, but—"

"It all depends on how the situation unfolds. For now, let's focus on resolving the immediate issue at hand." The exhaustion on Saeki's face let up slightly. "Colonel Kazama, do you believe you can persuade Shiba to join the Dione Project?"

"Probably not," Kazama responded immediately.

Even if it was possible, he wouldn't want to recommend that Tatsuya go to America.

"The military's relationship with Tatsuya hasn't been the best lately," he explained. "This is partly my own fault, but I would say our recent covert surveillance in Izu sparked the most mistrust."

"Indeed," Saeki said, "I am to blame for part of that as well. Would you say that convincing him to join the project is not only impossible, but it would also worsen our relationship with him?"

"Yes, I would."

"Then do you believe refusing the Ministry of Foreign Affairs' request would win Shiba's favor?"

"I'm not sure about that. Tatsuya won't participate in the Dione Project no matter what we do, so he wouldn't be particularly grateful either way. Our best move in this case is to simply do nothing."

"I see," Saeki said pensively.

Kazama stood silently in front of her desk, waiting for what she would say next.

"I will honor your advice," she concluded.

"So we'll be doing nothing?" Kazama asked her.

"Precisely. The Ministry of Foreign Affairs' request was unofficial and did not go through proper protocol. There is no harm in ignoring it."

Kazama suspected that this was what the major general had intended to do from the very beginning. She had simply called him in to see if there was any way to gain favor with Tatsuya by using the situation to their advantage.

"Good work today, Colonel," Saeki said.

"Ma'am." Kazama saluted and left the room.

He briefly considered informing Tatsuya about his conversation with Saeki but quickly dismissed the idea. The actions of the Ministry of Foreign Affairs and the National Defense Force held no significance for Tatsuya, and they would not help repair their relationship. Kazama *would* have to reach out to Tatsuya, however, if naming him the fourteenth Apostle became a realistic option.

Tatsuya had already gained unwanted fame on a global scale as Taurus Silver. He might not be as resistant to public exposure now as he was before. That said, Kazama doubted the high schooler wanted to be officially recognized as a strategic-class magician. The National Defense Force would need to be cautious moving forward, since offending Tatsuya wouldn't be wise. As things stood, Kazama and Tatsuya were already growing apart.

◇ ◇ ◇

The struggle between Tatsuya and Edward Clark wasn't confined to the Ministry of Foreign Affairs. Japan's Ministry of Industry was also grappling with pressure from the ruling party to choose a side. As their former name (Ministry of International Trade and Industry) suggested, trade relations were a critical area of their jurisdiction. The USNA still remained the most important global trading partner, so bureaucrats were keen on nipping any potential trade disputes in the bud. For them, any confrontation with the USNA over a civilian was no laughing matter. Deep down, they wanted nothing more than for Tatsuya to go to America as soon as possible.

However, that morning, the minister's office began exploring the legislative measures necessary to set up a magic stellar reactor energy plant. In other words, they seemed to be leaning toward not participating in the USNA's Dione Project.

Neither the Dione Project nor the magic stellar reactor energy plant plan were public projects, so the Japanese government had no obligation to participate in either one. Even the New Soviet Union, which was considered the USNA's current most cooperative ally, had expressed its support through the academy rather than the government. At this stage, even if the Japanese government maintained a neutral stance, the USNA could not openly criticize them.

Given that constructing these power plants was a domestic endeavor, it fell within the Ministry of Industry's jurisdiction. However, now that inquiries were coming explicitly from the minister's office, it seemed the government was feeling pressure to provide the plan with direct support.

The Ministry of Industry was already aware why this was happening. It turned out there were vested interests within the minister's office, specifically from several major corporate groups that provided significant funding for the ruling party.

While this didn't apply to the entire economic sector, it was likely that some business leaders opposed the plan so as not to damage relations with the USNA. In other words, a plan proposed by a mere First High student had escalated to the point where it was splitting the business community in half.

The ministry was perplexed. It was beyond them how Tatsuya

Shiba had managed to establish the connections necessary to bring in top business leaders seemingly out of nowhere to join his cause.

◇ ◇ ◇

Tatsuya remained in his seat until morning classes were over. Once he entered his senior year, he would have more specialized magic-related courses, but he would still have his share of general requirements. He needed to take the general classes he had missed during his absence at triple speed to catch up.

Unfortunately, the classwork he had missed was more than he could finish in half a day. Then again, Tatsuya didn't expect to catch up immediately. When lunchtime came around, he stood up from his seat.

"Tatsuya, would you like to have lunch toge—?"

Before Mizuki could finish her invitation, a boy's voice called out behind them.

"Shiba."

It was Tomitsuka.

"Mizuki, you can go ahead to the cafeteria," Tatsuya said and spun around to the boy. "What is it, Tomitsuka?"

Tomitsuka hesitated for a moment before donning a serious expression.

"I have something to talk to you about."

"Will it take a while?" Tatsuya asked half-heartedly.

"Probably."

"Then can we talk after school?" Tatsuya suggested, reluctant but amenable.

"I'd prefer to address this now," Tomitsuka insisted.

"Didn't you say it was going to take a while?"

"Well…yes…" Tomitsuka hesitated.

Just then, a hysterical voice spoke up.

"What's your problem, Shiba? Just hear him out."

It was Chiaki Hirakawa glaring angrily at Tatsuya.

"Hirakawa?!" Tomitsuka exclaimed, more surprised than Tatsuya himself.

"You don't have to be so rude!" Mizuki retaliated. "Tatsuya never said he wouldn't talk to Tomitsuka at all!"

Clearly, Mizuki had lingered in the classroom instead of going to the cafeteria as she was told.

"Calm down," Tatsuya said to avoid a fight between the two girls. "I'm going to speak to Tomitsuka now, so tell the others I'm sorry for not joining them for lunch."

"All right," Mizuki responded reluctantly.

She gave him a nod and left the classroom.

"Where do you want to talk?" Tatsuya asked Tomitsuka.

"Uh, the rooftop should be good."

Tatsuya raised his eyebrows in mild surprise. There would probably be other students on the rooftop, but if Tomitsuka was okay with this, that was his prerogative.

"Fine," Tatsuya said and walked out of the classroom.

"Thanks, Hirakawa," Tomitsuka whispered to Chiaki and quickly followed Tatsuya to the roof.

Contrary to Tatsuya's expectations, the rooftop was deserted. Tokyo had entered its rainy season the previous week, and the sky was currently overcast. Given the threat of rain, it wasn't that surprising students didn't want to spend their lunch outside.

There were a few benches in the area, but neither boy chose to sit down. They simply found a place to stand, facing each other.

"So what do you want to talk about?" Tatsuya asked Tomitsuka.

"...My mother collapsed the other day."

"Yeah, Miyuki told me she was hospitalized."

Tatsuya's apathetic tone irritated Tomitsuka to no end.

"I'm sorry that happened, but it's an issue between your mother and the Ministry of Foreign Affairs," Tatsuya continued callously. "I don't understand why you're complaining to me about it."

"How can you say that?!" Tomitsuka exclaimed angrily.

"I could say the same thing," Tatsuya retorted cynically. "You're the one who picked a fight with a younger girl."

There was an edge in Tatsuya's voice that made Tomitsuka flinch. He suddenly noticed the cold anger in the younger boy's eyes.

"So what do you want me to do?" Tatsuya continued. "Offer myself as a sacrifice for the sake of your mother's peace of mind?"

"I never said that!"

"But you want to give me to the USNA."

"You don't have to put it like that," Tomitsuka murmured. Tatsuya was much more bitter than he had expected. "I just believe the USNA's project will benefit magicians worldwide."

"Tomitsuka, do you really not understand the Dione Project's true goal?" Tatsuya asked in frustration.

Unaware that Tatsuya was deliberately letting his anger show, Tomitsuka turned meek.

"Its true goal?" he repeated.

"The USNA wants to drive magicians off Earth and confine them to the Jupiter Sphere, Asteroid Belt, and Venus Sphere," Tatsuya explained.

"What?"

"Magicians from the USNA, the New Soviet Union, and Britain will be stationed in permanent orbit. If I participate in the Dione Project, I could end up being sent to Jupiter's satellite orbit and unable to come back for over ten years. It could even mean exile for life."

Tatsuya paused before sarcastically adding, "You could even call it space exile."

But these last words didn't register with Tomitsuka.

"That...can't be right," Tomitsuka insisted weakly. "You're probably overthinking things."

"I'm not asking you to accept what I'm saying right away, but I recommend looking at the project's official documents yourself. If you still have doubts after that, come find me again."

With that, Tatsuya spun around and left. Tomitsuka didn't try to stop him. Even if Tomitsuka remained convinced the Dione Project was for a beneficial cause, Tatsuya had no intention of yielding. He wouldn't participate in the Dione Project. He refused to leave Miyuki on Earth and venture into space. That much was clear. His suggestion to review the project's documents was merely a tactic to buy time.

Meanwhile, Tatsuya also wanted Tomitsuka to recognize the corrupt side of the project on his own. Tomitsuka stood frozen in place even after Tatsuya was gone. It was only when a few drops of rain fell on his cheeks that he snapped back to reality.

"What the hell?" he whispered bitterly. "The Dione Project has ulterior motives to exile magicians to space? That sounds like a conspiracy theory to me."

But no matter how much Tomitsuka tried to fight them, Tatsuya's words had ingrained themselves in his mind. It soon started to pour. Yet the senior boy remained on the roof, indifferent to the rain.

"I never heard about that. No one even mentioned it."

To be precise, this was only true of the circles he interacted with. None of the programs he watched had mentioned the possibility. However, there were, of course, limits to the information one person could access. In the end, human beings could only rely on their own thoughts.

"There's no way there are ulterior motives involved," he insisted. "The public wouldn't allow that to go unannounced."

At the same time, no one's thoughts formed in a vacuum. They were inevitably shaped by the information a person encountered in their daily life. Tatsuya and Tomitsuka had very different experiences, absorbed different information, and ultimately held different opinions. Neither was better or worse than the other; they simply weren't the same. This was why Tatsuya's conclusion was difficult for Tomitsuka to accept.

Maybe Tomitsuka's perspective was typical of society overall. His resistance to accept what Tatsuya had told him was a more common reaction than Tatsuya may have thought.

◇ ◇ ◇

Since the failed attack on Izu, Edward Clark had been calling Bezobrazov nonstop, but he had yet to catch him.

"Still no luck with reaching Dr. Bezobrazov?" William MacLeod asked on the other side of the screen.

"Unfortunately not, Sir William," Clark replied.

It was past midnight in Clark's residence in LA and early morning in MacLeod's native London. Since they had no idea where Bezobrazov was, it was much harder to call him.

"I feel he is intent on avoiding us," Clark continued.

"Well, that can't be helped. Dr. Bezobrazov is from the opposite side of the world. I dare say it was impossible to control his actions from the very beginning."

"Do you think he wishes to attack Tatsuya again?"

"Most likely. He seems determined to destroy mass energy conversion magic by any means necessary with his own hands."

"I wish he had waited a little longer," Clark muttered, tousling his own hair in frustration. "Do you think he can do it?"

"I do," MacLeod replied hesitantly. *"However, I would say his chances are fifty-fifty. His last attempt seemed promising, but we also are not fully aware of the extent of Tatsuya Shiba's abilities."*

Despite MacLeod's uncertainty, Clark had to agree with him. "So you think it's up to Tatsuya's magic? I would say you're right."

"Could you use your Hlidskjalf to obtain information on the boy?"

"Unfortunately, they don't call him untouchable for nothing."

The Yotsuba clan had been known for their impenetrability for many years. Even before Tatsuya emerged into the spotlight, Clark had recognized the Yotsubas as adversaries he would need to deal with eventually. Truth be told, he gave Maya a Hlidskjalf terminal only with the ulterior motive to gather information on the clan as a whole.

Unfortunately, Maya was not exactly cooperative. Her search and input history revealed very little about the abilities of Tatsuya or any other family member, for that matter.

"I see." MacLeod heaved a disappointed sigh.

While this was not meant as a personal jab, Clark's pride took a significant hit.

"In that case, all we can do is hope Dr. Bezobrazov's next attack is successful. Good night, Dr. Clark. Apologies for keeping you up so late."

"No need to apologize. I was the one who called you. Thanks for answering so early in the morning."

"I am always awake at this hour." MacLeod smiled. *"Good evening, Doctor."*

"Have a good day." With that, Clark hung up the call.

Though MacLeod had told him to have a good evening, Clark doubted he would get a decent night's sleep.

[5]

From Tuesday to Thursday, there were no significant developments in either Japan or the world at large. On the outside, the conflict between Tatsuya and Edward Clark seemed to have reach a stalemate. Behind the scenes, however, Raymond Clark was steadily moving his own agenda forward.

On Saturday, June 15, the National Particle Accelerator Institute on the outskirts of Dallas, Texas, experienced more traffic than usual. Preparations for a secret experiment had been underway since that morning around the lab's massive, thirty-kilometer linear collider.

The experiment was based on a surplus dimension theory and involved micro black hole generation and evaporation. A similar experiment had been conducted in December 2095, to obtain clues on the workings of mass-energy conversion magic.

However, the objective this time was not to observe the energy generated by micro black hole evaporation. There was simply no need. The secret experiment's motive was to lure out suspected foreign infiltrators within the research facility.

That said, the scientists involved in the experiment saw it as a precious opportunity to revisit their previous results. Eager to make the most of it, they worked tirelessly in the short amount of preparation time they were granted. Dealing with the foreign infiltrators fell upon the shoulders of the present Stars teams.

If any infiltrators appeared, they were likely high-level magicians. This was all the more reason why the Stars were deployed. In fact, the Stars themselves were the ones who proposed that no other teams should be present.

Captain Alexander Arcturus, the commanding officer of the Stars' Team 3, was in charge of the security center that monitored all areas of the research facility. He was currently in communication with Lieutenant Jacob Regulus, a first-class member of the Team 3. Regulus was stationed in the laboratory's control room, watching closely for any suspicious activity.

"Anything out of the ordinary, Jake?" Arcturus asked.

"*Negative, Captain*," Regulus replied. "*There have been no sightings of anyone who appears to be an infiltrator.*"

"All right. Continue monitoring the area."

"*Roger that.*" Regulus saluted.

As soon as Arcturus paused his communication device, he was approached by a member of the constellation class. The Stars were divided into first, second, constellation, and satellite classes. This ranking system was separate from military ranks. It was not uncommon for constellation-class noncommissioned officers to operate under the command of satellite-class warrant officers.

"Captain," the constellation-class soldier said to Arcturus, saluting.

"What is it?"

"Are you sure Japan was involved in Lieutenant Fomalhaut's case? Frankly, I find it hard to believe that Japanese operatives would be capable of something like that."

Constellation-class soldiers had been stationed at the Dallas National Particle Accelerator Institute since Sunday, the day after the secret experiment was approved. Since there had been no trace of an enemy during all this time, the soldier's belated skepticism at this stage of the operation was understandable. To prevent his subordinate's morale from declining, Arcturus decided to disclose some less sensitive information.

"The Japanese military succeeded in developing autonomous humanoid weapons with parasites just last year," he stated.

"Really?" the soldier asked in surprise.

"Yes. And they seem to have been preparing for the project beforehand. While there is no direct evidence, their success alone is ample proof that the Japanese military was involved in the Lieutenant Fomalhaut incident."

There was a misunderstanding in Arcturus's deduction. Parasidolls, the autonomous weapons that used parasites, were originally created to run on *shikigami* magic techniques. However, while *shikigami* and artificial spirits could move the body, they couldn't fully utilize magic. Parasidolls weren't fully recognized until parasites came to be.

In other words, parasites were utilized only for weapons that had been on the verge of completion. What came to be known as Parasidolls were not initially developed with the use of parasites in mind.

The evidence Regulus received and then conveyed to Arcturus and Walker was distorted with fabricated circumstances added to surface-level facts. Regulus had then convinced his superiors of the involvement of Japanese operatives to carry out the micro black hole experiment once again.

"I had no idea. My apologies," the soldier said.

He did not question the legitimacy of this distorted information.

Little did the Stars know that an intruder had already entered the institute undetected. He had managed to do this thanks to a temporary staff pass issued by the National Science Bureau that he had obtained through his father's connections. The intruder, Raymond Clark, stood atop the rooftop of the laboratory's administrative building, gazing down at the magnificent accelerator.

Raymond was, in fact, the one who had fabricated the involvement of Japanese operatives to push for the reimplementation of the experiment. His goal was to summon parasites to counter Tatsuya. In other words, he exploited Regulus's desire for revenge for his own selfish purposes.

Still unable to come to terms with the brutal execution of his friend, Regulus finally found an outlet for his pent-up anger through this experiment. That alone was enough to allow him to be controlled like a puppet by Raymond's whims.

Both Regulus and Arcturus were far superior to Raymond. They were elite magicians belonging to the Stars, a group Raymond could never hope to reach. And yet the younger boy had managed to force them into a farce he had scripted himself. Raymond watched the scenario unfold as if it were a grand comedy.

However, a grave outcome awaited at the end of this performance, and Raymond had come to witness it firsthand. Seeing the results through Hlidskjalf wasn't enough. He was driven by an intense curiosity and need for instant gratification.

All the real staff members were completely immersed in the once-in-a-lifetime micro black hole experiment. None of them had time to reproach Raymond for simply leaning on the rooftop railing and watching the action below.

Once 11 AM rolled around, it was time to start the experiment. The Stars were not directly involved in the experiment itself. Regulus, who held his post in the control room, also refrained from interfering. Ultimately, he had no interest in whether the experiment succeeded or failed. His mind was entirely consumed by a hunger for revenge against those who had betrayed Fomalhaut. He wanted nothing more than to capture the operatives who'd incited the initial parasite experiment, uncover their masters, and crush them all.

As Regulus was focused on any suspicious behavior in the area, the head scientist signaled his team to start the accelerator. The machine sprang into motion while absorbing vast amounts of electrical power. A group of scientists injected both ends with proton beams, which spun in opposite directions along collision trajectories.

The experiment was over as soon as it had begun. This process was usually repeated multiple times until the scientists received their desired result. This time, however, there was no second attempt. There weren't any issues with the accelerator; the experiment simply succeeded on the first try.

Immediately after the head scientist signaled the start of the experiment, darkness enveloped Regulus's field of vision. For a moment, he thought there was a power outage. But soon, he was overwhelmed with an intense pain and pressure as if something was invading his body, trying to force its way inside him.

He intuitively understood this invasion wasn't physical. At the same time, the pain was completely different from any mental interference attacks he had experienced in training. It was probably the same kind of pain a woman might experience when losing her virginity, but of course, he wouldn't know.

Regulus struggled to push back whatever was invading his mind. The discomfort of the invasion of a foreign entity bothered him more than the pain itself. Unfortunately, he wasn't skilled in mental interference magic and didn't know how to manipulate his mind to chase the invader away. Instead, he tried psion manipulation, typeless magic, and even resorted to using his specialty emission-type magic to cast electric shocks on himself.

However, nothing he did proved effective against the intruder. The self-destructive lightning magic failed to cast. And so the intrusion continued.

Regulus didn't sense any will or intention from whatever it was that invaded him. All he felt was the entity slowly fusing with his sense of self. The invasion silently transformed into assimilation. Then the pain faded away. The pressure lessened.

Could this be a parasite?! Regulus thought.

Fear suddenly surged through his body. His consciousness screamed in terror. Then, like the dying glow of a candle, it steadily and quietly dimmed. The fear and anger he harbored against the phantom invader sank into the depths of his mind, leaving him with a sense of calm.

My name is Jacob Regulus.

The people of this world call me/us parasites.

And so Regulus became a parasite.

Right after the experiment was completed, Arcturus distinctly sensed something invading his mind.

Is this some kind of spirit? he wondered.

Unlike Regulus, he didn't experience any pain or pressure, thanks to his proficiency in spirit magic. Though he excelled in movement-type magic, he had also studied ancient magic, which involved summoning spirits into himself to harness their power. In modern terms, this was much like magicians conjuring beasts to channel their power.

Arcturus was accustomed to the sensation of something other than himself dwelling within him. Even when the being invaded his mind without consent, he remained unfazed. He knew how to deal with intrusions into his psyche.

The problem was that the intruder—the parasite—lacked a sense of self. Parasites had a mental presence beyond their host but were devoid of any will, making them indistinguishable from the host's own consciousness. The parasite entered Arcturus's mind without any particular intention, seeping like water into a dry cloth and penetrating Arcturus's core.

Once he realized the techniques he had mastered were ineffective against the intruder, fear began to sink in. He tried summoning a spirit to expel the intruder, but there was no response. At this point, the intruder had already crowded Arcturus's inner mind and fused with his sense of self.

The invasion had silently turned into assimilation. Arcturus suddenly felt fulfilled.

This is the true unity I sought but could never attain through summoning spirits, he thought before his consciousness faded into oblivion.

My name is Alexander Arcturus.

The people of this world call me/us parasites.

And so, Arcturus became a parasite.

"Ow, ow, ow."

Raymond was writhing on the administration tower rooftop.

"Ow, ow, ow, ow."

Only expressions of excruciating pain escaped his lips from the sensation that something was infiltrating his psyche. He had never been trained to resist mental interference–type magic, so the pain was more than he could bear. In fact, the pain was so overwhelming that he wasn't even aware of the oppressive sensation of something intruding his mind.

Yet Raymond's strong sense of self vehemently rejected the intrusion. This powerful resistance intensified the pain. At the same time, since he was unaware of his body's internal struggle, he couldn't do anything to stop it.

"Ow, ow, ow, ow, ow, ow!"

The relentless agony shattered Raymond's mind. Perhaps it was a blessing that his resistance was relenting. As his sense of self waned, the pace of the invasion accelerated. Raymond lost the strength to thrash around; he couldn't even yell out in pain anymore. Then, all of a sudden, he lay motionless on the rooftop.

His fading consciousness was like that of a dying body. The intrusion advanced rapidly, and assimilation progressed. Now unopposed, the entity invading his mind reshaped Raymond's will in its own image, and Raymond's will, in turn, imbued the entity with his essence.

* * *

Raymond knew he lacked the power it took to be a protagonist. Yet deep down, he longed for the role. He yearned to be a hero in his own epic saga, conquering the universe with magic. That, he thought, would make all his dreams come true.

Tatsuya Shiba stood in the way of Raymond's saga, denying its legitimacy. Yet the American boy knew that overpowering Tatsuya was impossible with his power alone. Even Sirius, the strongest Stars magician, wasn't strong enough to compete. So Raymond sought the power of parasites.

He believed if he could get a parasite to possess a Stars magician, he could bring Tatsuya Shiba to his knees. He had set the stage of Tatsuya's defeat at the hands of a parasite.

That is Raymond's/our desire.

Raymond/we wish to defeat Tatsuya Shiba.

My name is Raymond Clark.

The people of this world call me/us parasites.

Together, we will make Tatsuya Shiba succumb to our power.

The voices within Raymond's mind swore to make his twisted desires come true.

Parasites had been called into the world once more. Regulus, Arcturus, and Raymond were not the only ones whose minds they took over. The three members of the Stars' Team 6—the Orion Team, who had been waiting outside the building—had also become parasites.

After the experiment ended, the Stars-members-turned-parasites went back to their headquarters in New Mexico without anyone recognizing their internal transformation. Meanwhile, Raymond went back to his home in California as if nothing had changed.

◇ ◇ ◇

On Sunday, June 16, Minoru Kudou returned to the warehouse where the Parasidoll was stored. It was still before dawn, and the outside world was draped in darkness and silence. No one in Minoru's family would know where he was. His father, his brother, and the servants all assumed he was asleep in his room.

The previous day, no one had scolded him for skipping school to visit Minami in Tokyo and returning home the same day. Only Minoru's grandfather, Retsu, questioned him with a look of concern. But when Minoru explained the situation, his grandfather simply accepted it.

Minoru's father and brother were much more neglectful, making him think they had given up on him at this point. Maybe they misunderstood Minoru's actions as him finally giving up on life or decided to let him do as he pleased since he could die at any moment.

All things considered, Minoru was grateful for the misunderstanding. Every moment spent with his family and servants took him away from his goal. He wanted nothing more than to cure Minami, although he didn't fully understand why he was so passionate about it. Or maybe he did but chose not to acknowledge it. Maybe he wanted to believe his motivation wasn't merely driven by a shallow feeling of love at first sight that had awakened within him in the span of three days.

Unlike the last time he visited the warehouse, Minoru used an unlocking spell to open the doors. This spell used the Electron Goldworm spell he had learned from Gongjin Zhou. It was the same spell Xiangshan Chen used to infiltrate the Magic Association's Kanto branch. Minoru's version, however, was more refined than Chen's and didn't trigger any alarms.

The warehouse's cool, dry air enveloped Minoru's body as he entered. Again, there was no sign of spiritual energy.

"I guess this is the only way," Minoru murmured.

The voice within him didn't answer. He was speaking to himself, not Gongjin.

Minoru approached the coffin-like box at the back of the warehouse. Inside lay the frozen body of an East Asian man. It was one of the parasites Tatsuya and Mikihiko had sealed away the previous winter during an exercise in First High's forest. There had been both a real and a fake corpse, and this was the real one. The body's skin bore inscriptions and symbols designed to contain the parasite within.

This corpse served as the source of parasites used for Parasidolls. When the seal was partially relaxed, the parasite would escape and attempt to send out copies of itself to other bodies. These copies were then trapped within gynoids, and the corpse was sealed once again.

This was how the researchers of former Lab Nine, now known as Magic Technician Development Institute Nine, manufactured Parasidolls. Even though production had been suspended, a team of technicians updated the sealing program every twelve hours under the Kudou family's jurisdiction.

Since the last update time was 4 AM, the magic effects were starting to weaken. Minoru pressed a switch on the side of the coffin, causing the lid to open. Thankfully, the corpse was dressed in white robes. Minoru had no desire to see the body of a naked man, even if it was a corpse.

He placed his right hand on the corpse's chest, only to be met with a rigid sensation beneath his palm. Of course, there was no heartbeat. He then sent psions into the frozen body. After a few seconds, a surge of pushion waves responded as the dormant parasite within the corpse awakened.

Minoru swallowed hard. He clenched his teeth, pursed his lips tightly, and held his breath. After a moment of hesitation, he lifted the seal.

In a matter of seconds, a slime made of light burst out of the corpse.

Minoru's eyes widened in awe. Before him was a dimly glowing, shapeless entity of light. Size-wise, it was more like a slime than an amoeba. It lunged at Minoru, but he didn't dodge it. In fact, he held out his arms, almost inviting the parasite in.

A magic circle embedded in Minoru's light summer sweater lured the parasite. The parasite dove into the circle, as if being drawn in. Minoru groaned in agony at the intrusive sensation in his mind and dropped to the warehouse floor. Crossing his legs with his left foot atop his right thigh, he assumed a half-lotus pose. Despite the pain, he managed to maintain the pose and activate a cooling spell to soothe his discomfort.

The spell lowered his body temperature to mimic a corpse-like state. By turning his consciousness inward, he focused on maintaining control and suppressing any instinctual resistance to the parasite. His pseudo-death state served as a defense mechanism against the parasitic intrusion, allowing him to preserve command of his mind.

I will not lose to a creature without a conscience! Minoru thought.

He wielded the spell's program to subjugate the parasite without smothering it.

I will not lose this feeling! he shouted internally while engaging the parasite in battle. *How could throwing away my humanity be worth it if I lose even a fraction of how I feel?!*

Minoru had decided to become a parasite to save Minami from death and escape from his own vulnerable body. Still, he resisted the idea of abandoning his humanity.

Minoru had not succumbed to Gongjin Zhou's temptations. He simply wanted to become a parasite to confirm he could maintain his own soul and mind. His goal was to prove that even if a parasite invaded a human body, the heart could conquer it. This was the only way he would consider using the parasite method to treat Minami.

In other words, Minoru was sacrificing himself by using his own body as a guinea pig. He was offering his own flesh to gain demonic power. It could have been a decision born of the resignation that he didn't have much longer to live. But Minoru had a chance of success. Better yet, he was absolutely determined to succeed.

After acquiring Gongjin Zhou's knowledge, Minoru realized there was no other way. He had no choice but to make this method work. Failure was not an option. At times like these, strong conviction was his greatest weapon. Sometimes, technique could be the key to defeating spiritual entities. Miyuki's Cocytus, for example, was extremely effective at destroying fused parasites.

However, mere technique wasn't sufficient to control spirits. Parasites weren't like Gongjin Zhou's ghost—a remnant of a lost life. They were creatures that, though lacking material form, consumed and proliferated on their own. To tame it and house it within the human body, someone would need a mind too powerful for the parasite to devour. Blind determination convinced Minoru that he could do it. But it was a reckless gamble.

"Obey and become one with me!" Minoru roared, and all of a sudden, the assimilation process came to an end.

I am Minoru Kudou.

I hear a voice trying to connect with me.

It's whispering for us to become one.

But…

I am me, not "us."

Minoru had merged with the parasite but managed to remain himself. He put an end to the cooling spell on his body and rolled onto his back.

Thanks to the parasite's regenerative abilities, Minoru's frostbite healed quickly. He could sense that new organs had formed deep inside his forehead. It was an entirely unfamiliar phenomenon, but it had no noticeable impact on his consciousness as far as he could tell.

A chuckle bubbled up within him. Still lying on the warehouse floor, Minoru burst into gleeful laughter.

[6]

On the evening of Sunday, June 16, Miyuki went to visit Minami in the hospital. Just as she was about to leave, another visitor knocked at the door.

"Who is it?" Miyuki asked, standing up from her stool.

Minami looked terrified, but Miyuki gave her a reassuring pat on the shoulder and walked toward the door.

"It's Minoru Kudou," a voice said outside the room.

"Minoru?" Miyuki echoed.

She spun around to Minami, who nodded bashfully. Miyuki beamed despite herself.

"Coming," she said and opened the hospital room door, where Minoru stood an arm's length away.

It was hard to say whether it was fortunate or unfortunate that no one else was there to witness this. There stood two of the most heavenly beauties in the country. A painter might have offered up their soul just to capture this moment on canvas. A poet might have contemplated ending their life in despair after their words failed to accurately convey the scene. To the two subjects in question, however, their interaction felt mundanely normal.

"Welcome," Miyuki said to Minoru. "Are you here to see Minami?"

"Yes. Um, mind if I come in?"

"Of course." Miyuki stepped aside, letting him pass by her.

Minoru held a bouquet of red roses, pink gerbera, and orange carnations. Miyuki gave him some space so he could hand these flowers to Minami himself.

He held out the bouquet with a slight flush in his cheeks. Minami accepted them, blushing with her head down bashfully. Though Miyuki felt as if she could watch this sweet scene forever, she knew it wouldn't be fair, and she broke the ice instead.

"Thank you, Minoru. Where would you like to put them, Minami?"

The pair jolted in surprise, and it took Miyuki everything she had to suppress a laugh.

"Um…how about over there?" Minami replied, pointing to one of the bedside dressers.

Miyuki smiled as she took the bouquet and arranged the flowers according to Minami's wishes. Unable to stand the awkwardness, Minoru quickly changed the subject.

"Uh…is Tatsuya around?" he asked.

"Oh, were you hoping to see him, too?" Miyuki immediately replied.

It was unclear whether her quick answer was a way to help Minoru fill the silence, a knee-jerk reaction to hearing her fiancé's name, or a mixture of both.

"He just stepped out to the doctor's office," she told Minoru. "Is it an emergency?"

"Not really, but I would like to speak to him."

"About what?" a voice asked from the open doorway.

"There you are, Tatsuya!" Miyuki exclaimed. "Did you finish talking to the doctor?"

"Yeah, I got all my questions answered," Tatsuya said.

He walked into the room and shut the door. Miyuki had intentionally left the door open so she and Minami would not be alone with a boy.

"So, Minoru," Tatsuya began, narrowing his eyes involuntarily before putting on his usual poker face. "What did you want to talk to me about?"

Put on the spot, Minoru found it difficult to reply right away.

After a brief pause, he mustered up the courage to say, "It's about Minami's health."

"Okay, let's talk somewhere else," Tatsuya said.

"Wait!" Minami protested. "If you're going to talk about me, I would appreciate it if you did it in front of me."

"But…" Minoru trailed off hesitantly.

"Please!" Minami insisted. "I want to know the truth."

"All right," Minoru relented. "If you say so."

"Should I leave?" Miyuki asked.

Her question was posed to her fiancé, but Minoru answered instead.

"No, I think you should hear this, too."

Tatsuya pulled over a pair of stools for him and Minoru to sit on.

"All right. Take a seat," Tatsuya said.

With a fearful look on his face, Minoru did as he was told. Miyuki returned to the stool she had been sitting on, and Tatsuya sat down on a stool by her side. With Minoru at the foot of the bed, all four of them were facing each other. Minoru hesitated before he began speaking.

"I'm not sure what the doctor told you, but Minami's wounds are never going to completely heal."

His expression wasn't calm because he couldn't be. Miyuki seemed the most surprised by this news. Her hands flew to her mouth, and her eyes became as wide as saucers. Minami, on the other hand, maintained her composure, at least on the outside. Tatsuya simply gazed quietly at Minoru.

"You probably knew this already," Minoru said to Tatsuya.

"No, I didn't. And I don't agree. Our definitions of what it means to be completely healed are clearly not the same. You probably mean Minami's magic-calculation region will never be the same."

"Do you think everything is fine as long as her symptoms don't get worse?" Minoru asked.

"Not exactly, but there's no point in arguing about the details of our definitions. What's your point?"

"The bodies of engineered magicians are anything but stable."

"So you're afraid she might die suddenly?"

"That's right. There might not be anything wrong with her medically, but she could be gone tomorrow just like a sudden gust of wind puts out a flame." A shadow crossed Minoru's face. "This is now the life both Minami and I lead."

"How did you…?" Miyuki trailed off.

She meant to question how he knew Minami was an engineered magician, but she ended up simply staring at him in silence.

"In other words," Tatsuya interjected, "you're saying Minami's injuries to her magic-calculation region have increased her risk of sudden death."

"Yes." Minoru nodded. "Did you know about this risk, too?"

"I have looked into engineered magicians and their risk of sudden death. Someone who was basically family passed away under similar circumstances in the past."

"I…had no idea."

Minoru thought about offering his condolences but ultimately decided against it, feeling it would just sound superficial.

"Overheating the magic-calculation region damages the information bodies associated with the physical body," Tatsuya explained. "That damage then affects the physical form. Typically, the magic-calculation region's activity is limited enough to prevent self-destruction, but engineered magicians struggle with the effectiveness of their internal safety mechanisms. This is the hypothesis that seems to apply to Minami's situation."

"I agree," Minoru replied. "The only thing I would add is that overheating the magic-calculation region always involves a breakdown of a magician's safety mechanisms."

"Are you saying the destruction of safety mechanisms causes the overheating?"

"I don't know if it's the safety breaking that causes overheating or the process of overheating that causes the safety to break."

Despite the uncertainty of Minoru's words, there was no hesitation in his voice.

"But in this case, the exact mechanism doesn't really matter," he continued, staring Tatsuya straight in the eyes. "Either way, the safety is destroyed. That's what's important. Don't you think?"

"Yes, that's true," Tatsuya agreed wholeheartedly. "Are you worried Minami might suddenly be affected by an unintentional initiation of her magic-calculation region and suffer serious damage?"

"Exactly. Minami's current condition increases the likelihood of the tragedy all engineered magicians face becoming a reality."

"But I thought you said there was no way to repair the magic-calculation region," Tatsuya mused. "Or are the safety mechanisms a different story?"

When Minoru hesitated to respond, Tatsuya added, "Minoru, it sounds like you brought us a solution today."

Minoru looked down at the floor to escape Tatsuya's piercing gaze.

"...I did," he replied curtly.

"So what is it?"

"......"

"Minoru." Tatsuya stood up from his stool and took a half step sideways toward the bed as if to shield Miyuki and Minami. "What have you become?"

Minoru finally raised his head, his lips curling upward. Tatsuya didn't soon forget that smile. It was eerily similar to the one Gongjin Zhou had flashed at him in Kyoto.

"Does this answer your question?" Minoru asked.

Miyuki jumped to her feet. Even she recognized the unnerving psion waves that Minoru was suddenly emitting.

"Is that—a parasite?!" Miyuki gasped.

Minami simply stared wide-eyed. Though Tatsuya was standing between them, her eyes were fixed on Minoru.

"No need to worry," Minoru said, standing up from his own stool and flashing Miyuki and Tatsuya a smile that had lost all trace of Gongjin. "I'm a Kudou. We literally created Parasidolls. Besides, I'm the second-greatest magician after my grandfather. I've been trained in controlling parasites."

"There's one thing you have wrong," Tatsuya said.

Minoru furrowed his brow, confused by what this meant.

"You're not the second-greatest magician in your family," Tatsuya explained, completely solemn. "You're *the* greatest. In fact, you're the most prominent magician among all the twenty-eight families that have a *nine* in their name."

A genuine but somewhat soulless smile spread across Minoru's lips.

"That's nice of you to say," he told Tatsuya. "It means a lot to get a compliment from you."

But even this didn't make Tatsuya drop his guard. In fact, it made him as tense as ever.

Minoru, on the other hand, was utterly uninhibited.

"Oh, come on," he griped, his gaze flitting between Miyuki and Tatsuya. "There's no need to be so uptight. I might have a parasite inside, but I'm still me. My mind hasn't been possessed. I have no desire to attack humans, and I don't crave the things I used to lack."

"You say that, but you were human before," Tatsuya said. "Now you're a parasite."

"Well, that's true..." Minoru looked slightly hurt, but he quickly pulled himself together and continued speaking with conviction. "Really, though. I'm still me. I'm still Minoru Kudou. With the right knowledge and power, I believe humans can merge with parasites without being controlled by them. In fact, I'm living proof of that. Parasites don't need to be feared."

"You don't mean...," Tatsuya whispered, his voice low but clear. "Are you trying to turn Minami into a parasite, too?"

Miyuki suddenly whipped out the CAD in her handbag and stood on the defensive.

"Parasite bodies are very strong against psion waves," Minoru replied. The slight hesitation in his voice was viable proof that he hadn't changed. "If magicians merge with parasites, they won't ever have to worry about getting physically injured," Minoru continued. "In fact, since parasites are so similarly close to magic, magicians can be at peace knowing that their magic-calculation region will never act up again."

"Under regular circumstances, the right thing would be to ask Minami what she thinks," Tatsuya said, remaining firmly between Minami and Minoru. "However, as her employer, I would like to express my thoughts on this first."

Technically, Miyuki was Minami's employer, but there was no time to quibble right now. Tatsuya was compelled to say his piece.

"I'm sorry, but I won't allow you to turn Minami into a parasite," he told Minoru.

"What?!" Minoru was genuinely surprised that Tatsuya would be against his idea. "But at this rate, she could die at any second!"

"If her magic-calculation region is genuinely at the heart of her current illness, there are ways to help without turning her into a parasite."

"Still. It's impossible to restore her magic-calculation region completely. If there was at least a way to restore its safety function, I wouldn't be suggesting the parasite thing at all!"

"Safety function aside, it's possible to seal the magic-calculation region from the outside to avoid it ever going out of control again."

Minoru's eyes widened in disbelief, and he took a couple of steps backward. "In other words, you're planning to take away her magic?!"

For him, to take away a magician's magic was the same as taking away their very sense of self. Especially since Minoru had been raised knowing only the life of a magician, Tatsuya's suggestion sounded deplorable.

"I only want her to survive," Tatsuya said.

"Even if that means she's no longer a magician?!" Minoru countered.

"Humans can live without magic. She now has the option to live more peacefully as a normal girl."

"That's just what *you* want!" Minoru spat. "You have no right to take away her magic!"

"Sure, my solution would take away her magic. But, Minoru, don't you see? Your solution would take away her very humanity."

"Then Minami should decide! It's her life. If she's against becoming a parasite, I'm happy to walk away from the idea. So how about it?"

He called out to Minami, although Tatsuya still stood in the way of them making eye contact.

"I don't want you to die, Minami!" Minoru pleaded. "I don't want to take away your magic, either! Please—do what I did! Be like me!"

Minami looked hesitant. She had no intention of becoming a parasite. The decision to throw away her humanity entirely was not one she could make on a whim. She wasn't sure if she could give up her magic, either, but she thought it best for Tatsuya to take the reins here. At the same time, Minoru's words made her have second thoughts.

For better or for worse, Tatsuya's steeled voice was strong enough to interrupt those thoughts and dismiss Minoru entirely.

"I already told you," Tatsuya said. "The answer is no."

"Move aside, Tatsuya! I want to speak to Minami!" Minoru insisted. Anger had entered his voice.

Suddenly, he cast a spell. It was only a teleportation spell, lacking any acceleration or deceleration, to try to move past Tatsuya.

Yet in an instant, it reached top speed like an attack. Tatsuya's response was instinctual but precise. In an instant, he disintegrated Minoru's magic program with Program Dispersion.

"What are you trying to pull, Minoru?" Tatsuya demanded.

"Just shut up and get out of my way!"

He relied heavily on his prowess as a magician. Being unmatched in his magic abilities was what gave him a wellspring of confidence. The moment Tatsuya neutralized his magic, Minoru became angry and frantic.

The only time he had lost a battle was through forfeit. This lack of experience in defeat haunted him right now.

After having lived his whole life with a frail body, he was borderline obsessed with the "if onlys" of having perfect health. If only he were healthy, he would never lose in a magic battle. Yet that conviction was overturned in a matter of seconds.

Despite his sudden lack of composure, there were plenty of reasons to sympathize with the young, almost seventeen-year-old boy—if he had been normal. But Minoru wasn't normal. He wasn't even human anymore. He attacked Tatsuya with a stronger and faster spell this time.

Tatsuya suddenly shifted gears into the role of a merciless combat magician. After dismantling Minoru's second spell, he flew at the boy in one swift move.

His right palm pressed gently, almost tenderly, against Minoru's abdomen. Through this palm, a burst of magic surged forth—an acceleration spell at point-blank range. The spell didn't just affect Minoru's stomach, it propelled Minoru's entire body backward, sending it flying through the air.

Instead of slamming into the door, Minoru stopped midway and landed softly on the floor without a sound. Using Tatsuya's acceleration spell as a springboard, Minoru cast an acceleration spell on himself to neutralize the impact and effectively cancel out the force. This technique allowed him to move away from Tatsuya.

"Miyuki!" Tatsuya shouted before Minoru's feet could even touch the ground. "Cast a maximum interference field!"

"All right!"

As soon as Minoru landed, Miyuki's interference field enveloped the entire hospital room. Minoru glanced briefly at Minami before swiftly unlocking the door and flinging it open. By rushing out into the hallway before Tatsuya could get near him again, Minoru managed to escape the effective range of the interference field.

One of the hallway's closed windows shattered outward into the courtyard down below. Briefly meeting Tatsuya's gaze, Minoru leaped through the now glassless window. Tatsuya understood the meaning behind Minoru's glance.

"Miyuki. Stay by Minami's side," he ordered.

"What about you?"

"I'm going to fight Minoru."

Minoru didn't flee from Miyuki's interference field out of fear. He was simply worried that fighting in the hospital room could potentially cause unnecessary harm, and he didn't want to risk injuring Minami. To avoid this, he deliberately lured Tatsuya outside.

If Tatsuya stayed in the hospital room, Minoru would probably retreat for the day.

But the boy was very much attached to Minami. That much was painfully clear from their brief interaction. Even if he backed down now, he would surely come back.

Tatsuya's priority was to protect Miyuki. He couldn't afford to spend every waking hour at Minami's side. His best option was to render Minoru powerless so he was no longer a threat. Tatsuya followed Minoru through the shattered window and down into the hospital courtyard.

Minami's room was on the fourth floor. It wasn't impossible for Tatsuya to jump down with physical strength alone, but he didn't want to leave himself vulnerable after he landed. Minoru had long been an exceptional magician, even before he transformed into a parasite. Tatsuya summoned the inertia control program from his memory storage's magic program library.

Once both boys were in the courtyard, Minoru cast a Spark spell, but Tatsuya was quicker. His simultaneous activation of an inertia control magic through Flash Cast nullified and effectively countered Minoru's attack. Tatsuya also cast Program Dispersion within his artificial magic-calculation region to help counteract Minoru's spell.

"I knew you were using Program Dispersion," Minoru said calmly, his anger having clearly subsided. "I had my doubts back in the hospital room, but here we are. Only a Yotsuba could cast a spell in battle when it's barely succeeded in the labs."

"Your attacks reek of parasites," Tatsuya said. "They never hesitate to resort to unilateral displays of power for the sake of their fixations."

This unexpected reproach took Minoru off guard. His measured gaze flickered with agitation.

"You were never this self-conceited when you were a human," Tatsuya told him.

"I'm not self-conceited! And I did nothing wrong!"

He unleashed the Human Combustion spell, which forcibly extracted electrons from molecules responsible for cell regeneration and released them outside the body. Its name came from the emission it left on the skin, resembling spontaneous human combustion. However, it didn't actually cause people to explode. It simply destroyed the target's cells at the molecular level by depriving them of electrons required for intermolecular bonding.

Tatsuya neutralized the Human Combustion magic program just before it could activate. Even for him, this was a close call. The speed at which Minoru was casting spells was astonishing. He had always been quick at spell casting, but fusing with a parasite further enhanced his activation speed.

Unfortunately, Tatsuya's comment meant to unsettle Minoru had the opposite effect. Minoru's accuracy wasn't compromised at all. In fact, he seemed more stimulated—almost excited—since the activity of his magic-calculation region was heightened.

At this point, holding back was no longer an option. Tatsuya found himself reluctantly taking the confrontation seriously. When

Minoru first appeared in Minami's hospital room, Tatsuya had felt no hostility. If only he had been better at communicating.

But there was no time for regrets. Tatsuya unleashed another Dismantle spell without his CAD. Using CAD would have been moot against Minoru's speed. Had he not been released from Oath's seal, Tatsuya probably wouldn't have stood a chance.

The information body Dismantle spell hit Minoru, and he disappeared without a trace. A few seconds later, Minoru's true form reappeared unharmed to the right. The target Tatsuya had hit was an illusion created by the camouflage spell Parade. In other words, Tatsuya had only disintegrated a phantom.

He cast another spell, causing his perception of Minoru's location to shift from the right to the left, where his real body actually stood. Minoru had cast another spell called Qimen Dunjia, which deceived the opponent's perception of the caster's direction. Tatsuya quickly used Dismantle on this magic, too.

It looks like parasites aren't the only thing Minoru absorbed, he thought.

Former Lab Nine focused on integrating ancient magic techniques into modern magic. While it wasn't impossible that Qimen Dunjia was one of the old spells they researched, it couldn't have been the exact same program that Xiangshan Chen had used.

Each spell had its individuality. Even when two magicians used the same spell to achieve the same effect, subtle differences would arise in the casting process, especially if a magician made a mistake. The higher the perfection of the spell, the less noticeable these differences became.

Of course, this also depended on the power relationship between the caster and his opponent. Tatsuya's Third Eye could sense the individuality of Minoru's Qimen Dunjia. It was exactly in Gongjin Zhou's style.

When did he absorb Gongjin's spirit?

While Tatsuya pondered over this, magic sparks appeared in the sky. Minoru had cast the emission-type spell Cloudless Thunder. It ionized the air, creating a shower of extracted electrons. The negatively charged target would then be exposed to a surge of positive ions in a powerful two-stage attack.

Minoru unleashed this spell just as Tatsuya was in the process of using Dismantle on Parade and Qimen Dunjia. This time, Cloudless Thunder was faster than Tatsuya's magic program.

Tatsuya selected the program for Conduction Membrane from his library. This emission-type spell effectively reduced the electric resistance of the surface of clothing and shoes to zero, preparing them to defensively channel the electric current of lightning strikes into the ground.

Summoning the magic program into his artificial magic-calculation region, Tatsuya attempted to activate Conductive Membrane with Flash Cast. But before he could do that, a magic program causing an increase in electrical resistance was cast upon him. While this spell wasn't particularly powerful, it clashed with Conductive Membrane, causing both spells to fail.

Failing to activate a defensive spell in time led Tatsuya to be engulfed by Cloudless Thunder's electron shower. Suppressing a groan, he rolled himself across the hospital's natural grass lawn. Beneath the grass was a layer of earthy soil that absorbed the excess charge on Tatsuya's body along with any positive ions.

As Tatsuya rose to one knee Minoru stood frozen, his face betraying surprise. Even if Tatsuya could endure the pain, his muscles, bombarded by the electron shower, shouldn't be able to move freely.

This wasn't the result of Minoru's carelessness. He had simply been misled by what he considered reasonable. Blood spurted from the bottom of his right foot while his left suddenly lost feeling, causing him to fall backward and land flat on his back.

Tatsuya aimed to completely immobilize Minoru by targeting his shoulders and left leg. However, he soon realized that all he had on the ground was an empty shadow.

Just then, magic sparks appeared behind him, a sign that Cloudless

Thunder was about to begin. Without turning around, he swiftly diffused the spell with Program Dispersion. But his "eyes" weren't solely focused on the Cloudless Thunder. He searched for Minoru's presence in every direction.

Thanks to this hyperawareness, Tatsuya managed to destroy the Heat Blade—a spell that thinly compressed air to create a type of air projectile—that flew toward him from the right. Released by Tatsuya's Dismantle, the projectile rapidly expanded, triggering a huge gust of wind.

Since the ground was covered with grass, the strong wind didn't kick up dust to impair visibility, but it still made Tatsuya squint. With half-closed eyes, he struck the left side of the ground. Suddenly, he felt a faint sense of urgency in front of him. Minoru had unwittingly given himself away.

Tatsuya swiftly dispelled the lightning magic rising from the ground just before it took shape. He then dismantled the deceleration cage that would have restrained his movements immediately after the spell's activation. By neutralizing the compression of the air, he dispersed all the airborne projectiles as well. At this point, it was clear that each of Minoru's successive magic attacks was potentially lethal.

After neutralizing all the attacks, Tatsuya had Minoru within striking distance. He thrust out his right index finger in a technique known as *Ipponken*. His finger pierced Minoru's clothing and skin, boring a deep hole into the base of Minoru's left arm.

This attack wasn't the result of his training in karate or kenjutsu. Tatsuya had merely cast Mist Dispersion from his fingertip. If he had aimed at Minoru with his naked eye or magic vision, the attack would have been blocked by the Kudou family's secret technique, Parade. So he closed in until he was at point-blank range and unleashed zero-range Dismantle. This ensured that, even if all his senses were deceived, Tatsuya's attack would inflict damage if it hit his opponent's body.

Minoru screamed. He attempted to use his parasite's life force absorption ability, but Tatsuya withdrew his finger just in time.

Next, Tatsuya aimed his left index finger at the base of Minoru's right arm. Minoru didn't have time to react; another hole was drilled into his right shoulder. Tatsuya then pulled back.

However, Minoru counterattacked midway. His left hand, which should have been immobilized, suddenly grabbed Tatsuya's left wrist. A sudden sense of weakness overwhelmed Tatsuya. Minoru was draining something from him. It wasn't psions, but something akin to life energy. Minoru was using the parasite's ability to absorb vitality.

Luckily, the process was brief. Immediately after Minoru grabbed his left wrist, Tatsuya reflexively twisted his arm to break free from his opponent's grip. He then swung his right hand down like a knife, severing Minoru's left hand below the wrist. Minoru caught his left hand as it fell to the ground, and he jumped backward. Though he didn't exert much force into the jump, he managed to retreat an entire five meters.

He placed his severed left hand against the stump of his arm and left Tatsuya to marvel at the sight of its seamless reattachment in the blink of an eye. Minoru glanced at Tatsuya with a smirk. But despite his demeanor, there was not a trace of malevolence in Minoru's face.

"Is this your first time seeing parasite recuperation powers?" Minoru asked.

Tatsuya could think of only one previous example—the parasite who had infiltrated First High as an employee of Maximilian Devices, hiding among Lina's associates. That parasite, which Lina referred to as Mia, had swiftly healed a wound inflicted by Erica's blade, even after being pierced through the chest.

Upon closer inspection, not only had Minoru's severed wrist reattached, but the holes in his right leg, left shoulder, and right shoulder were also healed. He had clearly acquired the same ability as the parasite known as Mia.

"I see," Minoru said, gleaning the answer he was looking for from Tatsuya's subtle expressions. "I guess not all parasites are alike."

"Parasite abilities vary widely in type and level," Tatsuya said.

"You might have overcome your physical weakness by becoming a parasite, but there is no guarantee that Minami will heal in the same way."

Minoru gasped. Tatsuya took this opportunity to thrust his right fist forward. Using a technique he'd learned under Yakumo's guidance specifically for combating parasites, he unleashed the typeless magic Piercing Psion Bullet. The spell soared through the air, just as it was intended.

Psion Bullets could theoretically travel at any speed. With no mass and no physical form, they weren't even bound by the speed of light. However, Piercing Psion Bullets were no ordinary psion bullets. They weren't just hard; they also transcended the information dimension as they soared through the air.

Under usual circumstances, there was no concept of movement in the information dimension. While information that moved may have existed, any change in the information itself was discontinuous and instantaneous, requiring no time at all. All changes merely involved a rewriting of where the information would be applied, which could be done in less than a second.

The Piercing Psion Bullet introduced the concept of movement into that information dimension. It consisted of psions imbued with the definition of continuous and exclusive movement. As a result, its alternative path was limited within the magician's—in this case, Tatsuya's—movement perception. The bullet was also restricted to the speed at which Tatsuya could throw it himself. In short, it was regulated by Tatsuya's own physical limits.

Tatsuya's bullets could exceed 100 kilometers per hour, but their speed fell short of both regular bullets and arrows. This made it possible to track and evade them. As soon as Minoru caught sight of the Piercing Psion Bullet, he instinctively leaped toward the sky with a flight spell. The bullet pierced through his Parade illusion left in the information dimension and disappeared.

The flight spell Minoru used was not the same modern magic

spell that Tatsuya had developed. It was a flying program from the ancient magic system of Daoism. Minoru's spell condensed a cloud beneath his feet, imbued with stability, levitation, and horizontal movement, allowing him to speed through the air.

Tatsuya tried to dismantle the cloud, but Minoru didn't fall. This time, he used modern weighting magic to neutralize gravity and float in place. While flight magic was considered a major challenge for weighting magic, given the difficulties posed by free aerial movement, floating was a different story. Minoru extended his hands toward the ground and fired a series of plasma bullets from his palms.

Meanwhile, Tatsuya used a simple magic technique to compress air into ionized golf ball–sized spheres. While defensively thwarting plasma bullets or dispersing plasma in midair, he cast Mist Dispersion at Minoru.

Unfortunately, the spell failed to activate. Instead of floating in place, Minoru began moving through the air with a series of jumps. He still wasn't flying; he was simply leaping off self-created platforms while leaving behind mirages of himself with Parade. At this rate, capturing Minoru's true form was the least of Tatsuya's problems.

He faltered. Even if he managed to wound his opponent with Partial Dismantle, Minoru had his parasite healing abilities. To stop him, Tatsuya would have to knock him unconscious. But even severing his hand hadn't worked. Mist Dispersion was the only way. Then again, that would inevitably lead to Minoru's death. Tatsuya was hesitant to go that far.

Minoru's attacks, though potentially lethal, couldn't kill Tatsuya. Even with plasma bullets, he couldn't stop Tatsuya in his tracks. The real problem would be magic that went beyond his regeneration abilities and attacked his mind. Luckily, Minoru had not attempted to use mental interference magic so far. Maybe it was because he couldn't. Either way, his current magic repertoire didn't pose a real threat to Tatsuya.

Most importantly, Minoru had yet to aim at Miyuki. His focus was on Minami's treatment, so his hostility was probably temporary. He may have turned into a parasite, but he could potentially be useful in the future. The question was whether it was worth losing such a valuable asset here and now. This dilemma gave Tatsuya pause.

But at this rate, nothing will be resolved, he thought.

If he dismantled Minoru's body entirely, it might render the parasite regenerative abilities ineffective. Even if he didn't reduce the entire body to dust, dispelling the image of death might make the parasite retreat. He could also try dismantling Minoru's heart and quickly blowing away the parasite with Program Demolition. He could then regenerate Minoru's heart and return him to his human form.

Here goes nothing.

Just as Tatsuya prepared himself to put an end to the battle, Minoru stopped attacking.

"Do you have a feeling we've reached a stalemate?" he asked, as if reading Tatsuya's mind. "I don't think I can break through your defenses without killing you."

"I was thinking the same thing," Tatsuya said.

Minoru smiled. "I believe the best option to restore Minami's health is for her to become a parasite."

"I disagree."

"Yes, I know. Our opinions are like oil and water."

He looked up at the hospital window where he had jumped out.

"What's important is Minami heard what I think."

He glanced back down at Tatsuya.

"That's enough for me right now."

Minoru's body rose into the air. A cloud appeared again at his feet, and he rode it into the distance. Once Minoru had disappeared, Tatsuya sighed.

"He's gone."

Tatsuya knew this wasn't the end. Nothing had been solved yet.

Minoru would surely come again. But at least Tatsuya could rest a little easier knowing they were done for today.

◇ ◇ ◇

When Tatsuya returned to Minami's hospital room, he simply told her that Minoru had gone home. Area Interference disrupted magic casting, but it did not block magic waves. Miyuki's Area Interference was no different.

Even from a distance, Minami would have sensed Tatsuya and Minoru's intense battle. Yet she didn't ask for details. Tatsuya reported Minoru's attack to Maya from a hospital phone and requested increased security before returning home.

Since they had left Pixie at First High that Tuesday, she wasn't in the apartment. As soon as Tatsuya sat down on the living room sofa, Miyuki took it upon herself to bring him a cup of coffee. Tatsuya took a single sip before placing his cup back on the table. He felt exhausted, especially after Minoru's attack, which had briefly drained his energy.

Miyuki stood on the opposite side of the coffee table hugging an empty tray to her chest.

"Are you all right, Tatsuya?" she asked timidly.

"It was a tough fight," Tatsuya replied honestly, "but I'll be okay."

"Is Minoru stronger now that he is a parasite?"

"I think so. He was always quick at spell casting, but becoming a parasite has made him even faster. Plus, his new healing and regeneration abilities are a pain in the neck."

"He can regenerate on command?" Miyuki gasped.

"Yeah. Remember that parasite we fought at First High's school gates when Lina was here?"

"Yes. I believe Lina called her Mia. Come to think of it, she did have powerful self-healing abilities."

"Well, Minoru is as good if not better than that."

"Goodness. That sounds difficult," Miyuki whispered solemnly.

"But the parasite's abilities are the least of our worries," Tatsuya said. "We need to be especially cautious of his original power and the power of someone else."

"The power of someone else?" Miyuki echoed in confusion.

"That's right." Tatsuya nodded with an uncharacteristically grim expression. "Like me, Minoru has Elemental Sight. I had a feeling about it before, but he confirmed it for me today."

When Tatsuya had attempted to cast a spell using Flash Cast, Minoru nullified it with a counter-spell, which reversed the act of casting. This was no coincidence or lucky hit. Minoru had read the output of Tatsuya's magic program.

"Oh!" Miyuki gasped.

She didn't seem either surprised by or suspicious of her brother's claim. If Tatsuya was sure, it had to be true. She only had one question: "Then…is the other person you mentioned…who I think it is?"

"Yes. I'm not sure how he did it, but Minoru has absorbed all of Gongjin Zhou's knowledge and abilities."

No matter how surreal this sounded, Tatsuya knew it to be true.

"By Gongjin Zhou, do you mean the man we fought in Kyoto?" Miyuki asked to confirm.

"One and the same."

"Did Minoru find some kind of document Gongjin had left behind and gain the abilities from there?"

That seemed like the most rational reasoning, but Tatsuya knew it wasn't true. He shook his head.

"No. In simple terms, I'm almost certain Minoru absorbed Gongjin's ghost."

With one arm hugging the coffee tray to her chest, Miyuki had only one hand free to fly to her mouth in surprise.

"I had no idea the Kudou family was capable of that kind of magic," she said.

But Tatsuya shook his head. "They aren't. Spells used to merge the human body with spirits are unusual, to say the least. They have completely different objectives from modern magic. That said, there might be a spell aimed to control spiritual entities."

Tatsuya paused to think of a concrete example for Miyuki to understand.

"Take Parasidolls, for instance," he began. "To complete them, magic must be used to control their parasite core. Minoru might have adapted this type of magic and incorporated Gongjin's ghost into himself in this way. Either way, his use of Gongjin's Qimen Dunjia was a dead giveaway."

"I see...," Miyuki whispered.

To be honest, she found it hard to believe Minoru could have incorporated the spirit of a deceased magician into his body. She accepted it as fact only because Tatsuya had said it.

"We have to come up with a plan to fight back. Dealing with a combination of old Lab Nine's magic, ancient magic from China, and parasite abilities won't be easy using conventional methods." Tatsuya furrowed his brow. "On top of all that, we have to inform Lord Kudou about his son. If Aunt Maya doesn't mention it, I'll have to bring it up myself. We'll need the Kudou family's support if we want to stop Minoru."

With the need to allocate resources to counter the Dione Project already weighing heavily on his shoulders, the Minoru situation only made things worse. No wonder Tatsuya felt gloomy. Miyuki looked at him with concern.

◇ ◇ ◇

Luckily, Tatsuya's worry that Maya might suppress the information about Minoru turned out to be for nothing.

It was Monday, June 17, the day after Tatsuya and Minoru's unfortunate battle at the hospital in Chofu. Tatsuya had been called to the Magic Association's Kanto branch. Only this time, their aim was not to convince him to join the Dione Project. He was requested to attend the ad hoc meeting of magician families as an observer—or better yet, as a witness.

Only Tatsuya and Katsuto were physically present in the conference room of the Magic Association's Kanto branch in Yokohama Bay Hills Tower. Katsuto treated Tatsuya as a representative of the Yotsuba family and interacted with him in a professional manner.

In fact, he acted like their battle on the last Sunday of the previous month hadn't even happened. At the same time, this unaffected behavior proved that he hadn't fully processed what had happened yet. Either way, both Tatsuya and Katsuto were distant toward each other.

The ten faces of the Ten Master Clan heads appeared on the screen before them. Katsuto was, of course, the in-person exception, and Retsu Kudou stood in for his son Makoto. The members swiftly went through the bare minimum of formalities before diving straight into the agenda. Gouki Ichijou, who had recently recovered from his illness, was the first one to speak.

"*It isn't as if I don't trust you. I just wanted to confirm*," he said in a hearty tone aimed at Tatsuya. "*Is it true that Minoru Kudou has become a parasite?*"

"That's what he said," Tatsuya replied. "From our battle, I could tell he was telling the truth."

The members on the screen displayed three types of emotions. Some looked surprised, some displayed no emotion at all, and others sadly lowered their eyes.

"*Is it also true that Minoru went to see Minami Sakurai, a magician under the Yotsuba clan's care?*" asked Gen Mitsuya, one of the surprised members.

"Yes. He also confirmed this himself."

"*Do Minoru and Minami have some sort of...special relationship?*" Takumi Shippou inquired.

"I'm not sure," Tatsuya replied.

The truth was that he had not confirmed the feelings of either party. If asked directly, Minami would probably have given the same answer as Tatsuya. It was highly likely that she was still confused about her feelings toward Minoru.

"*Let's put Minoru's motives aside*," Kouichi Saegusa cut in. "*While I believe the fact that he has set his sights on a member of the Yotsuba clan is certainly an issue, I am most curious about where he could have become possessed by a parasite.*"

"*That's a good point, Saegusa*," Isami Itsuwa agreed. "*Whether parasites have somehow made their way back into Japan or they were reborn within the country itself, this is an issue that we cannot ignore without facing real consequences.*"

"*About that...*," Retsu Kudou began bitterly.

But before he could finish his sentence, Tatsuya interrupted.

"The last time we were faced with an invasion, my friends helped me seal away two parasites. At the time, we were unsure how to destroy them, and they were ultimately stolen from us. I believe Minoru's parasite came from these two."

"*And you have no idea who could have stolen them?*" Kouichi pressed.

"That's correct," Tatsuya replied without hesitation.

"*You never carried out an investigation?*"

"Tokyo is not Yotsuba clan territory, so no."

Tatsuya's reply caused Kouichi to frown.

"The people involved in the incident were Mayumi Saegusa, Erika Chiba, and the Juumonji clan," Tatsuya continued. "All of us shared information about the stolen parasites."

"Yes, I heard about that," Katsuto said, speaking as the head of the Juumonji clan.

At this point, Kouichi had no choice but to back down. If Mayumi was involved, the Saegusa clan had to take some of the responsibility for what happened.

Just then, Maya spoke up unexpectedly.

"*One of the parasites is in my possession*," she said. "*I took care of it while Tatsuya was in battle with the other one. However, I was never able to locate that second parasite once it was sealed."*

"Why didn't you tell Tatsuya about this?" Mai Futatsugi asked in disbelief.

"I wanted him to focus on his studies," Maya said reproachfully. It was clear to everyone in the room that this was a brazen lie, but she continued to pretend otherwise. *"I had our parasite examined when Tatsuya told me about Minoru, but it seemed to be untouched."*

"Does that mean there is a strong possibility that Minoru was infected by the other parasite that went missing?" Atsuko Mutsuzuka wondered.

"Let's not jump to conclusions now," Raizou Yatsushiro cautioned. *"We're lacking too much information. Saegusa and Itsuwa's worries are valid, but I believe we should focus on handling what we know."*

Atsuko nodded. *"I couldn't agree more."*

In other words, Raizou was suggesting that they concentrate their efforts on Minoru. *"My apologies, Sage,"* said Raizou, *"but now that we are certain your grandson has been possessed by a parasite, we can't just let him run free."*

"I understand." Retsu nodded, clearly suppressing his emotions.

As the head of the Kudou family and Minoru's father, Makoto Kudou might not have been able to be so calm. Retsu was attending the current meeting ostensibly because Makoto was busy with internal family matters. But the truth could be that Makoto would have found it much harder to negotiate.

"There have been confirmed cases of parasites seeking new targets after losing their original host," Tatsuya added.

Though everyone present should have known this, their expressions revealed that they needed the reminder.

"Does this mean we should mobilize magicians capable of attacking spiritual entities?" Gouki asked.

"It would be much safer to try to render Minoru powerless without killing him," Takumi suggested.

Gen nodded. *"I agree."*

"*Tatsuya, do you know how to seal a parasite?*" Isami asked through the screen.

Before Tatsuya could answer, Retsu spoke up.

"I can tell you that."

"*You can?*" Isami said in surprise.

"*Excuse my forwardness, Sage,*" Gouki began, his gaze palpably suspicious. *"But where did you learn how to seal a parasite?"*

"*It's no secret,*" Maya interrupted. *"He is the one who taught us the program to seal parasites in the first place."*

The sternness immediately faded from Gouki's face.

"*I'd like to consult Sage for guidance regarding Minoru's capture. In the meantime, let's focus on devising a plan,*" Mai said, steering the conversation back on track just as it started to lose momentum. *"Is it safe to say Minoru is after Minami Sakurai?"*

"Yes, I believe Minami is his ultimate target," Tatsuya confirmed.

"*Then our most effective move would be to set up a trap at the facility where Minami is hospitalized,*" Gouki suggested.

He seemed to have no qualms about using Minami as bait. Interestingly, Maya didn't fight back.

"*Excellent idea,*" she said. *"I will make sure Minami is fully protected."*

In a way, it sounded like she was indirectly rejecting any help from the Saegusa clan. This made Kouichi frown.

"Ms. Yotsuba, the Juumonji clan would like to support your efforts," Katsuto offered, although it was unclear whether he was reading the room correctly.

"All right. As long as you remain outside the hospital."

"That's fine with us."

"Then we would be happy to accept your help."

That concluded Maya and Katsuto's exchange, which kept Kouichi out of the loop.

"*What should the rest of us do?*" Atsuko asked.

"*Minoru may have his sights on Minami Sakurai, but there is also a chance he may return to the Kudou family residence,*" Takumi replied.

Minoru had been missing since the day before. Takumi reasoned that though the boy had not gone home yet, he could show up at any moment.

"*I will of course catch him if he shows up here,*" Retsu said. "*We have no intention of hiding him.*"

"*That's not what we're worried about,*" Mai reassured him. "*Despite his poor health, Minoru has always been an excellent magician. Now that he has become a parasite, there is no telling how much his powers have grown. If you would like, I can send some of the Futatsugi clan to help handle him.*"

"*My family would be happy to help, as well,*" Gouki added.

"*I appreciate that.*" Retsu bowed his head. "*For the time being, I will take you up on your offer, Ms. Futatsugi. If we need more support, I will be sure to let you know, Mr. Ichijou.*"

"*Great,*" said Mai.

"*Understood,*" said Gouki.

"Then to summarize," Katsuto began, "the Yotsuba clan will oversee Minami Sakurai's protection. The Saegusa clan will lay a trap in case Minoru stops by. The Juumonji clan will provide protection from the outside of the hospital. The Futatsugi and Ichijou clans will provide support at the Kudou clan's residence. In the meantime, all other families will keep a lookout for Minoru. Does that sound good?"

A series of positive voices assented from the screen. The Ten Master Clan's policy regarding the Minoru incident was settled.

◇ ◇ ◇

Once a group of Magic Association personnel had come into the room to clean, Tatsuya and Katsuto headed to the elevators. Rather than walk side by side, Tatsuya walked at an angle slightly behind Katsuto to avoid being in Katsuto's blind spot. The older boy didn't explicitly request this; it was simply Tatsuya's way of being thoughtful.

The two did not speak. They simply walked forward in silence. No one could blame them. Their battle the previous month had been so fierce that one of them could have died under regular circumstances. Not enough time had passed to mend their relationship. The fact that they were able to hide their enmity toward each other was praiseworthy enough. Perhaps it was proof that they were mature enough to leave that sort of thing on the battlefield. Their silence was only broken by an abrupt voice from the corner of the elevator hall.

"Is the meeting over?" Mayumi asked casually, despite her involvement in the previous month's battle.

"Saegusa?" Katsuto said in surprise. "What are you doing here?"

"I was curious."

Katsuto rubbed his temple. Tatsuya knew exactly how he felt.

"Yes, the meeting is over," Katsuto told Mayumi.

"That was fast. So what happened?"

Katsuto was about to tell her to ask her father about it but stopped himself midway. He knew Mayumi much too well to think something like that would make her back down.

"We can't talk here," he said instead.

"Then let's find a meeting room."

Much like the Kyoto branch, the Magic Association's Kanto branch building had a number of rooms that personnel and approved guests could use to avoid being overheard. Though Mayumi wasn't exactly a regular, she frequented some of these rooms.

"You should come, too, Tatsuya," she urged.

Tatsuya knew Mayumi wouldn't take no for an answer. He had no plans for after the meeting, and there was still plenty of time before Miyuki left school. Although he wasn't thrilled about the idea of having to spend more time with Katsuto and Mayumi, he nodded and said, "Fine."

As soon as they entered the meeting room, Mayumi grabbed the kettle.

"Would you like some tea, Tatsuya?" she asked.

"Sure."

He noticed that Mayumi didn't bother asking Katsuto if he wanted tea. Tatsuya felt tempted to speculate about what this could mean, but he stopped himself after foreseeing the hassle it would entail. Mayumi placed three teacups on the table and took a seat across from Katsuto and next to Tatsuya.

"Drink up before it gets cold," she said.

Tatsuya and Katsuto interpreted this as a passive-aggressive order and they both took a sip. Mayumi's tea had become much tastier than when she used to make it in high school. Seemingly pleased with her own work, Mayumi happily set her cup down on the table. Once Katsuto and Tatsuya had done the same, Katsuto looked at Mayumi.

"What do you want to know?" he asked.

"Everything."

"Do you know what the meeting was about?"

"How to deal with Minoru turning into a parasite, right?" Mayumi replied instantly.

Tatsuya noticed that she was being awfully laid-back about the situation, despite knowing what had happened. Apparently, he wasn't the only one.

"Do you really understand what's going on?" Katsuto asked. "I thought you and Minoru were pretty close."

"Of course I understand," Mayumi said calmly. "I was involved in the previous parasite incident, too, you know. Although I ended up not being very helpful."

She sounded slightly disappointed at the end of her reply, but otherwise, she was the picture of serenity.

"In that case, you can probably guess what happened at the meeting," Tatsuya cut in.

"Sure," Mayumi said. "The goal is to capture Minoru and either seal him away or extract the parasite, right? What I want to know is how exactly you plan on catching him."

Katsuto and Tatsuya exchanged glances as if to make sure they could tell her and decide who would be the one to speak first. In the end, Katsuto decided to take the initiative.

"We're going to set up a trap at the hospital where Minami Sakurai is staying," he explained.

"Are you in charge?" Mayumi asked.

"No, your father is."

"My…father?"

A look of surprise broke her calm expression for a moment, but she quickly forced her lips into a polite smile.

"Isn't Minami one of Kasumi's classmates?" she continued.

"Yes, that's right," Tatsuya answered politely.

"So you're going to use a high school girl as bait? And you're okay with that?" Mayumi shot Tatsuya an accusatory look.

"Whether we like it or not, Minoru will visit Minami again," he told her.

"The Yotsuba clan will be providing protection inside the hospital while the Juumonji clan provides protection outside," Katsuto added. "We won't let Minami get hurt."

"I doubt Minoru would just waltz in with all that security in place," Mayumi countered.

"Then we'll just think of something else," Katsuto replied offhandedly.

"If you say so…" Mayumi sounded doubtful. "Either way, you and Tatsuya are going to join forces to solve this?"

Unsure what she meant by this, Katsuto frowned. But Tatsuya smiled inwardly. He understood she was just trying to help their relationship.

"As members of the Ten Master Clans, the Juumonji and Yotsuba families will always be allies," he explained. "A temporary disagreement isn't going to end that."

"If you say so…," Mayumi repeated.

But unlike before, a smile spread across her lips.

[7]

The outskirts of Roswell, New Mexico, in the United States of North America were home to the official Stars base. The Stars were divided into twelve teams, each of which followed their own orders. As the Stars commander, Lina needed to know about all the missions that each unit was conducting. Unfortunately, there were many missions she was not informed about.

The previous Sirius had complete control over the Stars, but Lina wasn't yet at that level. In fact, she was far from it. Sometimes, people would complain she was just a commander in name, and that criticism wasn't entirely unfounded.

Alone in her room, Lina took another shower, changed into her pajamas, and began murmuring to herself in bed.

"All teams were present today except for 3 and 6. Those two suddenly went MIA last weekend. At least I wasn't the only one who didn't know where they were, but this is getting out of hand."

On Saturday morning, Team 3's Arcturus and Team 6's Rigel went missing. As soon as Lina found out, she quickly contacted Canopus, who was usually so informed about each team's actions, you would think he was the Stars commander. Unfortunately, in this case he also had no idea where Arcturus and Rigel could be.

On the one hand, Canopus's lack of knowledge helped console

Lina that she wasn't the only one being kept out of the information loop. On the other hand, the fact that the Stars commander was left so uninformed remained a serious issue that bothered Lina to no end. She usually swept this source of stress to the back of her mind. But tonight it seemed to stubbornly cling to the front of her skull. No matter how hard she tried not to dwell on it, it kept repeating itself in her head.

Where in the world did Team 3 and Team 6 go? she thought. *And what are they doing? They should have at least told me the purpose of their mission.*

She knew it shouldn't bother her, but it was annoying her to no end.

Am I really just a commander in name, she mourned, *prized only for my strength as a strategic magician?*

The strength she was referring to was not the *power* to achieve goals but merely the brute *force* to knock down obstacles. Lina grimaced cynically at the thought that she was only recognized for this force.

"Maybe they're right," she grumbled. "I'm only seventeen, and I'm not a genius in any way. My grades weren't even that good in school, I was never properly trained for this job, and to top it all off, I'm short and have a baby face."

Her own pessimism sent her into a negative spiral. Rationally, she knew this self-pity was unhealthy, but she couldn't stop herself.

"Still. The least they could do would be to tell me why they were leaving. They can't just leave without telling anyone. If plans change, the repercussions will fall on my shoulders," she continued to herself. "If they're not satisfied with me as their commander, I'm happy to step down at any time. Excuse me for being unreliable. It's not like I wanted this position in the first place."

Lina pulled her blanket over her head and used a voice command to turn off the lights. Even if there was no one to listen, sometimes venting her frustrations out loud like this could bring a sense of relief. Besides, she was tired of struggling in the swamps of self-deprecation.

* * *

That night, Lina had a familiar dream. On the surface, it wasn't a particularly pleasant memory. It involved the time she infiltrated First High and had to kill parasites one after the other on the mountainside. She spotted a parasite and pierced its throat from behind with a knife infused with teleportation magic. Another parasite lunged at her, and she blasted it away with bullets of ionized air.

She found a parasite and used magic to shoot it down. Another parasite lunged at her, and she used magic to shoot it down, too. Before she knew it, the dream had started to loop. Defeating all these parasites felt like playing a zombie shooting game. Lina shook her head.

When are Tatsuya and Miyuki going to show up? she wondered, finding herself in the complex position of both an active participant and a spectator within her dream.

On the day she infiltrated First High, Lina remembered fighting alongside Tatsuya and his friends. In fact, she couldn't forget it. Though she resented being rescued in the end against her will, fighting alongside comrades on equal terms wasn't a bad experience at all.

Actually, given that they were supposed to be enemies, Lina couldn't shake the feeling that Tatsuya looked down on her. Yet neither Tatsuya nor Miyuki ever treated her like a little kid. They also never treated her differently just because she was one of the Thirteen Apostles.

Their behavior might have come naturally to them since they were all similar ages, but it really meant a lot to Lina. Then again, unbeknownst to her at the time, Tatsuya was a strategic magician with abilities that far surpassed Heavy Metal Burst. This was all the more reason for him not to treat her differently. Yet even knowing that now, Lina could still appreciate being treated as an equal back then.

While in Japan, she couldn't admit to harboring these feelings. But now that she was in an environment surrounded by older subordinates, she gradually became more open to acknowledging them. That said, she might still put up a stubborn front if she were to face Tatsuya again.

Without Miyuki and Tatsuya by her side, Lina felt a tinge of loneliness as she continued to fend off parasites. The only thing that kept her going was the need to distract herself from that empty feeling.

◇ ◇ ◇

In the darkness of the night, a beelike buzzing sound echoed through the air. The sound wasn't audible to the physical ear. It was a conversation only privy to spiritual forms—the voices of parasites discussing, questioning, and answering themselves.

We cannot permeate the commander's psyche.

We didn't know she was skilled in mental-type magic.

As far as we know, that should not be the case.

Then why can't we permeate her psyche?

She keeps pushing us back.

She's repelling us.

We are being forced to retreat.

Merging with her is proving a challenge.

It's impossible.

The commander is more dangerous than we thought.

She is.

We feel she will become our enemy.

We must dispose of her.

Yes, we will.

After a while, the two animated voices became one.

◇ ◇ ◇

It was not even 5 AM on Tuesday, June 18. As long as they weren't on a mission, even military personnel were asleep at this hour. Yet Lina suddenly found herself awake, and she pushed herself up in bed.

"Did that dream wake me up…?" she murmured to herself.

She vaguely remembered what it was about. It had not been a

good dream, but she felt it had helped her release some stress. She felt much lighter than when she had fallen asleep.

Lina had never been much of a morning person. Recently, she had gotten in the habit of pouring herself a cup of bitter coffee brewed by her home automation system to force herself awake, but she didn't feel the need for it this day.

It was June now. During the day, the temperatures often rose far above eighty degrees Fahrenheit, but before dawn, it remained around sixty degrees at the highest.

Perfect weather for a walk, Lina thought, then she quickly jumped out of bed.

Of course, she wasn't about to leave her room without making herself look presentable first. There were loads of things to do. Even though she wasn't currently on a mission, it was important to always be prepared.

By the time she was ready, the first light of day had graced the sky. Yet there was hardly anyone moving around the base grounds. That's not to say it was empty. There were soldiers on watch duty and maintenance workers who were up and about. Lina mentally acknowledged their efforts with a silent "thank you" as she made her way around the training grounds toward the fence that separated the base from the outside world.

This was the heartland of the USNA. The hands of armed separatists didn't reach this far. Unlike in conflict zones, there shouldn't be any need to worry about sniper fire around the fence.

The threat to Lina's life arrived silently. She managed to evade the invisible line of sniper fire purely by luck. In fact, she didn't completely avoid it. The high-energy laser pierced through her illusion and burned the fence from the inside. If Lina hadn't happened to deploy Parade a yard away from herself during her walk through the grounds, the sniper attack would have killed her immediately.

What shocked her the most wasn't narrowly escaping death.

She was, of course, genuinely relieved to have survived. A chill ran down her spine when she realized she was a sniper's target. But what truly shook her was the fact that the attack had come from inside the base.

"A mutiny?!" Lina exclaimed.

She immediately used teleportation magic to deflect the approaching missiles while establishing a magic barrier to block the heat and debris. At the same time, she traced the trajectory of the sniper's shot to a nearby warehouse rooftop.

"Jack?!" she shouted in surprise. "I knew it!"

A man was positioned on the rooftop holding something resembling a rifle. The distance from Lina to the warehouse was over a hundred meters. The sky was still dimly lit, making it difficult to identify the man with the naked eye. However, the psion waves he was giving off were unmistakably those of a familiar Stars member.

Lina recognized him as Lieutenant Jacob Regulus, also known as Jack, of Team 3. His specialty technique was Laser Sniping, which involved firing high-energy infrared laser bullets from a rifle-like device. Lina could tell that she was under attack by Laser Sniping.

"Jack! Why are you aiming at me?!" she screamed.

Jack didn't answer. Lina sensed an increase in magic and swiftly deployed the electromagnetic wave reflection spell, Mirror Shield. The shield effectively reflected Laser Sniping's attack. Laser Sniping was a silent and munitionless sniping magic, ideal for stealth attacks. Its only drawback was that it required approximately one second to charge before firing, not for the activation of the magic itself, but to amplify the light used as ammunition. This delay gave Lina time to deploy a shield right after sensing the magic activation.

While Mirror Shield reflected all incoming electromagnetic waves, including visible light, it also obscured the opponent's presence while it was deployed. As soon as Lina deactivated the shield, Regulus had disappeared from the rooftop. She raised her magic detection to the highest level and scanned the warehouse. Before long, she sensed a magic projectile imbued with Dancing Blaze, a spell shared among Stars combat magicians. Lina gasped.

"Huh?"

The psion waves embedded in this Dancing Blaze spell belonged to Captain Alexander Arcturus, known as Alex. Lina quickly cast Area Interference. Rather than setting it up around herself, she directed it at four incoming knives. The knives, which had been flying toward Lina in swirling curves, lost control and were hurled to the ground.

"So even Alex from Team 3 is involved in this mutiny," Lina muttered. "If I can even call it that."

She considered the possibility that the two men were attacking her due to a personal grudge. But she was too afraid to put it into words. It was too overwhelming for a seventeen-year-old to think about.

Lina knew she was in an enviable position, but she thought she got along well enough with everyone in Stars. Sure. Team 4's Vega and Deneb were notorious for complaining about her behind her back, but Lina never thought they were serious.

There was no time for wallowing in self-pity. Another Dancing Blaze came flying her way. This time, it was one flame instead of four, but the potency was far greater than earlier.

Is that a tomahawk?! Lina gasped to herself.

Area Interference wasn't enough to stop this attack.

Arcturus had a mix of white, black, and indigenous ancestry. In fact, the indigenous side made up a quarter of his heritage, and it showed up strongly in his magic. He used a technique found widely in ancient magic, where weapons were infused with a wish to magically enhance them and render them impervious to others' magic. This technique was also prevalent in Native American magic.

Arcturus had mastered a version with a tomahawk, and this was his trump card in battles against magicians. While it could be used in close combat, Arcturus primarily threw it from a distance using movement-type magic. His attacks were so powerful that not even Lina's Area Interference stood a chance.

Knowing this, Lina swiftly dodged nearly twenty meters sideways in one smooth motion. As soon as she landed, she redeployed Mirror Shield. Feeling the impact of the light bullets on her shield, Lina immediately ran for cover.

Although there were obstacles and shooting targets scattered around, this was still open ground and offered very good visibility. In fact, here, she made an even better target. That was why Lina darted into the special vehicles warehouse.

Special vehicles, in this context, didn't refer to heavy machinery or tanks. They were more like magic-fueled experimental weapons, such as self-propelled cars capable of short-distance flight, vans designed for underwater travel, or motorcycles that transformed into powered exoskeletons when integrated with a riding suit. Many of these vehicles sacrificed practicality for innovation.

Lina had heard there would be a long-distance test for a self-propelled car this very day. The warehouse door was likely open because maintenance personnel were going in and out to prepare for that test.

"This is Major Sirius!" Lina announced. "Everyone in the area evacuate immediately!"

As soon as she rolled into the warehouse, Lina was enveloped in the illusion of Angie Sirius.

"I'm glad I'm wearing my training field uniform," she muttered to herself.

She knew the feminine clothes she had collected under Silvia's guidance would have been utterly unsuitable in this situation.

She carefully scanned her surroundings, sharpening her senses to avoid overlooking anything and becoming a target. She appeared calm and composed, handling the situation with ease. But in reality, her mental state was far from calm.

She regretted bringing her personal information terminal instead of her commander terminal when leaving her room, but there was no use crying over spilled milk. Since it was still outside working hours, this wouldn't have been a problem if all hell had not broken loose. Not being able to reach base headquarters as a result was rough, but unavoidable.

The fact that she didn't notice the phone on the wall right above her head, however, could have been avoided. If only she had noticed it and reached out to headquarters for help. That simple action alone could have completely changed the course of events.

Lina focused on the area outside the warehouse, but there was no sign of Arcturus. She also considered the possibility that her enemies were not limited to just Regulus and Arcturus. By sheer chance, she noticed a grenade behind her and dodged just in time. The walls of the warehouse withstood the explosion, but Lina was showered with debris.

Using a magic shield, she managed to protect herself from both the explosion and its aftermath. Once things had settled down, she spun around to identify her attacker. It was Layla Deneb, a first-class lieutenant from Stars Team 4. The tall and glamorous woman of Nordic descent glared at Lina with intense hatred.

"Layla!" Lina gasped. "Not you, too!"

"Don't 'Layla' me, traitor!" Deneb snarled.

"Traitor? What are you talking about?"

"Stop playing dumb," Deneb scoffed, brandishing a knife in her right hand. "You really don't know when to give up."

In a matter of seconds, she appeared in front of Lina's pre-transformation state, standing taller and more voluptuous than Lina could ever be.

Lina instinctively cast a teleportation spell as Deneb's combat knife swung down upon her. In an instant, she reappeared on the opposite side of the warehouse entrance. The area echoed with the sounds of suppressed gunfire hitting the floor and Lina's shield.

Deneb clicked her tongue in frustration. The combination of knife and handgun magic was her specialty. This attack reminded Lina of that.

"I'm not playing dumb!" Lina yelled with her shield still up. "When was I ever a traitor?"

"You're shameless," Deneb spat. "I guess I'll just have to spell it out for you. You're the Stars commander, and yet you sold out Team 6 for the sake of a Japanese man!"

"Team 6? What does Randy's team have to do with any of this?"

"I see you're not ready to apologize," a voice called out behind her.

Lina quickly spun around and deflected another of Deneb's bullets. Thankfully, her shield's event interference was more powerful than the piercing spell on Deneb's bullets, designed to spear directly through obstacles.

Unfortunately, a simultaneous attack by a new enemy came from an unexpected direction. Both Lina and her shield were launched into the air. This wasn't a movement or acceleration spell; it was localized gravity inversion magic. The area around Lina experienced a sudden reversal and amplification of gravity.

The magic slammed Lina into the warehouse ceiling with ten times the acceleration of free fall. But rather than breaking, the ceiling only vibrated slightly in response to the powerful force. In a split second, Lina had instinctively neutralized her own inertia.

This proved effective, but it wasn't without consequences. Lina still experienced a powerful impact to her back before falling to the ground. While enduring the pain, she cast a deceleration spell on herself and managed to return to earth without suffering further harm.

She also managed to scatter a series of air bullets around her as she fell. Though lacking in lethal force, they served well as a distraction. Lina steadied herself upon landing and glared at Captain Charlotte Vega—the culprit who had slammed her against the ceiling.

"Char...," Lina said weakly.

"Interesting." Vega smirked. "I thought you were a goner, but I should have known you wouldn't go down so easily. I gotta give it to you, Commander. That magic of yours is the only thing that lives up to your name."

At this point, Lina's Parade had been dispelled, leaving behind a young girl with vibrant blond hair and blue eyes who struggled for breath. Vega's lips curled into a triumphant smile.

"Then again," she continued, "you seem out of breath. Serves you right for selling out your fellow Stars for the sake of a man."

"I didn't sell anyone out!" Lina protested. "What happened to Team 6? Who is this man you all keep talking about?"

"You still don't get it?!" Deneb shouted angrily.

Before she could fly into a rage, Vega stopped her.

"Fine. I'll tell you," Deneb said condescendingly. "I hereby accuse you of colluding with Japanese operatives to coercively reinstate the macro black hole experiment. As a result, three members of Team 6 fell victim to Japan's human experimentation agenda. And to think you did all this for the strategic magician Tatsuya Shiba!"

"Tatsuya?" Lina echoed incredulously.

She felt ridiculously and unjustly accused, but Vega and Deneb read her tone as undeniable proof of her betrayal.

"That's right," Vega said. "Randy, Ian, and Sam were rescued in a state of madness last night. They claim they were possessed by parasites because of you!"

Randy (Captain Orlando Rigel), Ian (Second Lieutenant Ian Bellatrix), and Sam (Second Lieutenant Samuel Alnilam) were all members of Stars Team 6, nicknamed the Orion Team. With their names still fresh on her tongue, Vega glared at Lina.

"They turned into parasites?" Lina asked in disbelief.

Unfortunately, this, too, looked like brazen acting in Vega's eyes.

"Traitors deserve death!" she claimed. "I'll give you the same fate you sentenced your fellow soldiers!"

Lina quickly regained her composure, but it wasn't quick enough. The shock of hearing about Team 6 was too great. She found herself facing Vega with her back to the entrance. From outside the warehouse, Arcturus's spinning tomahawk flew toward Lina's vulnerable spine.

Just as the attack was about to breach the warehouse, the fifty-meter, magically enhanced molecular blade sliced through the tomahawk. A large figure suddenly appeared at the warehouse entrance.

"Are you all right, Commander?" it asked.

"Ben!" Lina exclaimed.

"Lieutenant Canopus," Vega muttered. "Are you allies with the traitor?"

"Commander Sirius isn't a traitor, Captain Vega," Canopus said firmly. "The parasites are playing with your mind."

"What are you talking about?" Vega asked. "I never interacted with Randy's group."

"That's not what I mean! The parasites are—"

Before Canopus could finish, Lina simultaneously deflected a high-energy laser attack and redirected the incoming tomahawk with one fluid motion.

Just then, a screeching sound echoed through the warehouse. The experimental vehicle and subject of today's test run suddenly charged toward Lina and Vega. Reacting swiftly, they both leaped out of the way. The vehicle then veered off course and came to an abrupt stop as its right front door flung open.

"Get in, Commander!"

"Hardy?!"

Second lieutenant of Stars Team 1, Ralph Hardy Milfak, motioned Lina into the passenger seat. Without hesitation, Lina jumped into the car, and Milfak veered the driving console to the left.

This experimental vehicle was designed for both left-hand drive, as in countries such as the USNA, and right-hand drive, as in the UK. It featured a movable driving console that could veer left or right, and the front seats were seamlessly connected without a partition. There were also no pedals. As soon as Lina closed the door, Milfak sped away.

"I'm taking us out of the base!" he said.

"What?" Lina asked, puzzled by this announcement from out of the blue.

"Commander Canopus's orders!"

At this point, Lina trusted Canopus more than anything, so she didn't fight back. There was no time to fight back anyhow.

The vehicle they were in was shaped like a pickup truck. Suddenly, a loud thunk echoed from its rear. Adept at acceleration magic, Deneb used a pseudo-teleportation spell to leap into the truck bed.

"Wait!" she yelled.

"No can do!" a voice countered.

A young man who had been hiding in the back leaped at Deneb, causing them to tumble out together.

"Ralph!" Lina exclaimed.

She recognized the young man who had tumbled out of the truck as Ralph Algol, another second-rank lieutenant from Stars Team 1.

"We'll have to leave Deneb to Algol," Milfak said. "Now, hold on tight! It's gonna be a bumpy ride!"

Lina quickly fastened her seat belt, and the pickup truck flew down the road. Once they were past the base's fence, Milfak continued in the direction of Albuquerque. Lina felt much calmer once the base was out of sight. She turned toward Milfak.

"What in the world is going on?"

"Sometime around five in the morning, Captain Arcturus and Lieutenant Regulus of Team 3 incited a rebellion. Currently, the other known members of the rebellion include Captain Vega and Lieutenant Spica from Team 4; Captain Rigel, Second Lieutenant Bellatrix, and Second Lieutenant Alnilam from Team 6; and Lieutenant Antares and Captain Sargas from Team 11."

"Hold on!" Lina interjected. "Char said the members of Team 6 were possessed by parasites. Tell me that was a lie."

"Unfortunately, there is enough evidence to prove it's true," Milfak said. "And it's not just Team 6. There is a strong chance the two members I just mentioned from Teams 3 and 11 have also turned into parasites."

"I can't believe this."

"Lieutenant Shaula of Team 11 was the one who told us the news. She noticed Lieutenant Antares and Captain Sargas were acting strangely and reported it to Commander Canopus."

Team 11 was proficient in mental interference magic, but Second Lieutenant Shaula had exceptional sensitivity to psion waves and a strong defense against mental interference. It was undoubtedly thanks to her abilities that she remained unaffected by the parasites and managed to detect their presence.

"But, well...," Milfak said cautiously, "Shaula only reported to Canopus since you weren't in your room."

Milfak seemed to worry that Lina's feelings might be hurt, but Lina didn't mind. In fact, she didn't even notice.

"After Lieutenant Algol and I received emergency summonses, Lieutenant Antares activated Hypnos Garden," Milfak continued. "This saved us from Shaula's Lunar Eclipse, but everyone else in the dormitory was incapacitated."

Antares's Hypnos Garden was a type of exotype magic that induced sleep within a particular area. Since it targeted a wide range at once, it wasn't particularly powerful. In other words, it couldn't put soldiers in a worked-up state to sleep. However, it was effective at preventing people from waking up and at inducing sleep in those who had recently waken up or were fatigued.

Second Lieutenant Shaula's Lunar Eclipse was a defensive magic that utilized mental interference magic—known as "lunar magic" in the USNA—to disrupt the target's psychological perception and render their attacks ineffective. It was undoubtedly thanks to this spell that Shaula had avoided being invaded by a parasite.

"So what now?" Lina asked apprehensively.

She was used to relying on the Stars' backup for every operation, but that was clearly impossible now. At this rate, she worried about having to face a satellite-class magician without any equipment or funding.

As if in response to her worries, a notification sounded from Milfak's breast pocket. He switched the vehicle to autopilot and pulled out his device.

His fingers flew across the device's screen as if deciphering a complex encryption. After finally cracking the code, he read the message with a stern expression. Once he was done, he handed the device to Lina.

"Orders from Colonel Balance."

As soon as Lina took the terminal, Milfak went back to driving.

"After learning about the attack by Team 3, Canopus immediately consulted Colonel Balance for advice," he explained.

Lina took a deep breath and looked down at Milfak's terminal. As she read the colonel's email, her eyes became as round as saucers. Balance's orders were for Lina to seek exile in Japan under the Yotsuba family's protection.

"She wants me to go to Japan?!" Lina exclaimed. "But why?"

She couldn't fathom why she had to leave the States and go all the way to Japan.

"She probably worries you've become the target of a conspiracy," Milfak explained. "I doubt anyone in the Stars would go as far as assassinating a strategic magician, but there may be factions interested in manipulating you for their own purposes."

Lina suddenly recalled the military aircraft she found aboard the *Enterprise*.

Those magicians were being forced to use magic as a power source and treated as mere cogs in the military system, she thought. *Are there people who think of me as a piece of machinery, too?*

Given the current state of the world, losing Heavy Metal Burst was almost tantamount to national suicide. Brainwashing Lina into a more compliant pawn, however, could definitely prove valuable from a military standpoint.

"But wouldn't my fleeing to Japan make me a deserter?" Lina asked.

"I don't think you have to worry about that, Commander. Take a look at the attached file."

Lina quickly turned back to the terminal. Like the email, the attached file was also heavily coded. The contents consisted of an official order to infiltrate Japan for a clandestine audit of the military attaché stationed there.

"She's giving me an official order?!" Lina gasped.

"Colonel Balance did her best to facilitate your escape within the scope of her authority," Milfak said.

Balance was second-in-command in the audit department overseeing military misconduct. While fraught with technicalities, sending Lina to Japan for the sake of military officers working at the embassy and consulate could arguably—albeit just barely—fall within her authority.

"You can hold on to that terminal," Milfak continued. "Don't worry. It doesn't contain any of my personal information. I use the same password as Team 1."

As Stars commander, Lina had been granted permission to censor each team's information documents. Most people, however, ignored her authority, and Lina never brought it up as an issue. Only Canopus and Capella from Team 5 ever faithfully reported to Lina each time they changed their passwords.

"I put your passport, credit cards, debit cards, and various other equipment for the undercover mission in the carrier bag on the back seat," Milfak said. "Since you'll be traveling, you won't find any armed devices. Also, I didn't have time to provide a change of clothes, so please purchase those at the airport when we arrive. Colonel Balance already purchased your flight tickets."

Lina looked down at the terminal again. Sure enough, her virtual ticket had been forwarded to her.

"I'm driving us directly to the Albuquerque airport," Milfak told her. "Captain Canopus is holding the Stars off, so I don't think anyone is tracking us, but I'm using an anti-detection shield just in case. As an extra precaution, I suggest refraining from using magic until you reach your destination."

"All right."

Milfak's anti-detection magic was top-notch among the Stars. Even the tracking experts in Team 6, the Orion Team, would find the vehicle difficult to detect.

◇ ◇ ◇

Lina arrived safely in Japan on the afternoon of June 17, local time. She immediately called the number Balance had given her and was quickly put in the care of the Kuroba family, one of Maya's strongest allies.

Meanwhile, at the Stars base, Canopus, Algol, and Shaula had been sentenced in an informal trial to a military prison for magicians on Midway Island. Rather than returning to the base, Milfak escaped to the West Coast.

[8]

While the mutiny among the Stars was happening in the USNA, emergency repairs were being conducted on Bezobrazov's large Argan CAD in the New Soviet Union.

"How is it going?" Bezobrazov asked.

"Doctor!" one of the workers exclaimed in surprise, spinning around.

Being a scholar and an aristocrat, Bezobrazov rarely showed his face at greasy repair sites like this one.

"The repairs will be finished by the end of the day. We would be honored if you could give it a test run tomorrow," the worker said.

Bezobrazov was a government official akin to a military general, hence the worker's overly tense and formal tone. In other words, Bezobrazov wielded a fair amount of authority and influence in his country.

"That shouldn't be a problem," Bezobrazov replied. "What time do you want me to stop by?"

He had never wielded power or arrogance over ordinary people, especially technicians who didn't hold any official position. This wasn't because he was a man of high moral character; he simply couldn't care less about those beneath him.

"We should be ready for you as early as tomorrow morning!" the worker confirmed.

"All right. I'll be here at nine thirty."

"We'll be waiting."

Bezobrazov bade farewell to supervisors and technicians alike before leaving the maintenance facility. His rare visit was primarily because of the urgency he felt to use Argan again, but it was also driven by the humiliation he had suffered at Tatsuya's hands.

He had been so confident that the surprise Tuman Bomba attack would be a success. Yet he had failed to assassinate Tatsuya despite his use of Igroks, Tuman Bomba's special biological amplifier. Not only had he failed, but both Igroks used in the attack had been annihilated, and Argan had been rendered unusable. If it weren't for the Igroks, Bezobrazov's confidence would have probably been his end.

The New Soviet scientist had never failed as a strategic magician before. In the intense but small-scale battle against the USNA across the Berlin Strait, he had even managed to exterminate the previous Stars commander, William Sirius, with Tuman Bomba. His failure in the most recent mission felt like a terrible loss. He wanted nothing more but to resume operations as soon as possible to redeem himself from this humiliation.

◇ ◇ ◇

It was raining in Tokyo on the morning of Thursday, June 20. The area around First High in Hachioji was soaked from the steady rain.

Since it was the rainy season, the gloominess was inevitable. Most students seemed to take it in stride, but Tatsuya spent the morning on high alert. He only vaguely responded to Mizuki's curious looks, making no effort to conceal his anxiety.

Tokyo had been experiencing less precipitation than usual this year. While the first half of the month saw plenty of rain, it had been a while since there had been such continuous rain since morning. The recent intermittent rain didn't necessarily signal a break in the rainy season, but there had been fewer rainy days than average.

This didn't bother Tatsuya. In fact, he welcomed the absence of rain. He wasn't fond of rain to begin with, but he was particularly weary of it since returning from Izu. It had been raining the day he was targeted by strategic magic. A day of continuous light rain with no wind provided optimal weather conditions for Tuman Bomba.

This day, too, there was almost no wind. Tatsuya speculated if Bezobrazov were going to make a move, it would be today. Bezobrazov hadn't given up. Tatsuya was certain of that. The magicians he had eradicated eleven days ago weren't Bezobrazov, but he had a feeling they weren't completely unrelated.

It was possible that Bezobrazov was not the only wielder of Tuman Bomba. The New Soviet Union could be producing spare magicians for him. Even among the publicly known Thirteen Apostles, there were two strategic magicians in the USNA who wielded Leviathan, one in the UK and one in Germany who could cast Ozone Circle, and two in the Indo-Persian Federation who were proficient in Agni Downburst.

It wasn't uncommon for magicians to share strategic-magic programs. Because of the spells' immense destructive power, magicians with potential from the same country were actively taught how to wield them. In Tuman Bomba's case, however, Tatsuya felt that its activation was closely linked to Bezobrazov.

The two magicians Tatsuya had destroyed in the Izu Highlands had exactly the same genetic material. While they could be identical twins, Tatsuya suspected they were clones. There were distortions in their information structure that were more unnatural—or even more artificial—than were usually found in engineered bodies.

At the time of the attack, Tatsuya believed that Bezobrazov was Tuman Bomba's caster and the two female magicians were merely his tools. He later remembered, however, that Raymond Clark knew he could cast Material Burst. It was highly likely that Clark had conveyed this information to the New Soviet Union.

Tatsuya concluded that the attack on the villa in Izu was the result of the New Soviet Union's decision to completely neutralize his strategic magic, specifically his use of Material Burst. In fact, he believed that they had decided to eliminate him because he was a strategic-class magician.

Tatsuya had told Miyuki about his worries earlier that morning. He had also instructed Pixie, who had been reconnected to the First High system, to be on maximum alert. Then, just three minutes before the end of the last morning class, as Class 3-E was quietly studying on their terminals, Tatsuya sensed signs of an incoming attack.

◇ ◇ ◇

Bezobrazov sat in the operator's seat of his large Argan CAD, which had just undergone a series of minor modifications. It was midafternoon where he was and morning in Japan. The clocks in the coastal regions of the New Soviet Union were an hour ahead of Japan Standard Time. Though it was lunchtime for Bezobrazov, he paid no attention to the dining table and focused solely on the operation at hand.

Taking lessons from the previous encounter, Argan was improved to withstand Tatsuya's decomposition spell by using Igrok's molecular bond neutralization magic. This time, the New Siberian Railroad train car connected to Argan was also parked on the outskirts of Ussuriysk, north of Vladivostok rather than on the outskirts of Vladivostok itself, to avoid being targeted with the same geographic information as before.

Another change from the last battle was that Bezobrazov had brought in five Igroks this time rather than two. In other words, all the remaining Igroks were being deployed for this operation. Two would be used for activation, one would serve as an emergency firewall, and the last two were spares.

Bezobrazov had not put this much effort into his attack on the Stars. This alone proved his deep investment in this avenging mission. In the last battle with Tatsuya, he had ultimately tumbled out of the train car in fear of Tatsuya's retaliation. The memory of that moment gnawed at Bezobrazov's pride. He had to redress that humiliation as soon as possible.

He realized that doing nothing would make him go mad. The only way to forget the dreadful humiliation he suffered was to kill Tatsuya Shiba. This obsession had now taken root in Bezobrazov's consciousness.

He brought up the data from the intelligence department on his console. According to the coordinates, Tatsuya was currently at First High. Bezobrazov couldn't fathom what someone with the intellect to plan a fusion reactor plant could learn from high school. It seemed like a waste of time.

Academics aside, the fact that Tatsuya was inside First High posed a problem. The school's sturdily reinforced concrete buildings would be difficult to destroy with shock waves. They were made of high-strength materials developed during World War III, making them all the more resilient. Even breaking the glass windows wouldn't cause much damage.

Then again, Tuman Bomba wasn't suited for moving targets, and satellite imagery revealed Tatsuya's home building to be even sturdier than the school. Bezobrazov decided to shatter First High's windows with shock waves, allow the mist from the rain to infiltrate the school's interior, and trigger explosions from within. He retrieved this plan from his storage and began to prepare.

Bezobrazov's chair was slowly drawn into Argan's internal cavity. The strategic magician operated the switches on the console like a music conductor with his baton. Igroks served as his performers as they prepared to play a symphony of ruin and slaughter.

◇ ◇ ◇

"Master, magical activity detected two hundred meters directly above First High," Pixie warned telepathically.

Tatsuya had already suggested activating Chain Cast, which

replicated magic programs to trigger a series of spells with a shortened delay. He stood up and drew a large handgun-shaped CAD from his pocket.

Class was still in session, but he ignored his startled and whispering classmates. He then looked up at the ceiling and aimed his Silver Horn Custom Trident CAD directly above his head. There was no hesitation in his movements. Timing it perfectly to the second, he pulled Trident's trigger.

◇ ◇ ◇

A jarring alarm echoed inside the large Argan CAD. A warning message appeared on its inner console that the Igrok intended for Tuman Bomba activation had been eradicated in a fraction of a second during the spell's initial stage.

A magician's job was to construct magic programs. Even if the program was completed in the magician's magic-calculation region, the spell would not activate until it was fixed to its target's coordinates. If the magician happened to die the moment the magic program was fixed, the spell would fail to activate.

"Transfer over to the next Igrok," Bezobrazov ordered. "Hurry."

There was no escape this time. The New Soviet scientist anxiously awaited the exchange process, fearing the eerie specter of death looming over him.

◇ ◇ ◇

It was not easy to prevent Tuman Bomba from activating. More precisely, it proved challenging to neutralize a Chain Cast Tuman Bomba with Program Dispersion. Tatsuya had realized this after his two encounters with the spell.

The magic programs deployed by Chain Cast were each slightly different, and their differences became more significant as their coordinates diverged. Even if Tatsuya tried to break them down in groups, it was impossible to eliminate all the programs at once. Moreover, attempting to counter the programs with rapid-fire Program Dispersion ran the risk of Tuman Bomba activating in the process, exposing Tatsuya to a powerful explosion.

The only option was to completely stop the spell's activation. In his previous battle with Bezobrazov, Tatsuya figured out how to trace Tuman Bomba back to where it was cast. The moment Chain Cast began, he would trace its magical path and use Trident to decompose the caster into three parts. This was Tatsuya's strategy.

Chain Cast was a technique that simultaneously activated all magic programs after copying and fixing them to a specific target. Since it cast magic programs over a broad area, it was faster to use Trident to destroy a single entity rather than to trying to eliminate the countless programs. Even if the caster was two people, the attack would fall within a margin of error. But this wasn't a gamble; it was a defensive counterattack based on unmistakable odds.

◇ ◇ ◇

"Igrok transfer complete," a worker announced.

Without responding, Bezobrazov stared at the satellite imagery on his console. Since Tuman Bomba had just failed to activate, there was no change in the atmospheric conditions above the target. Rain continued to fall from warm clouds, and there was hardly any wind. Another attack could be launched soon.

In their previous battle, Tatsuya did not release a second wave of magic to neutralize any intermolecular bonding after eliminating two Igroks. A simulation of what it would have looked like if he had cast that magic proved that it would take over five minutes for Argan alone. It was that complex.

With only a handheld CAD at his disposal, there was no way Tatsuya could work at such blistering speeds. Even if he could,

Bezobrazov calculated it would take a significant amount of time. In that time, Tuman Bomba could be cast first. As a precaution, Bezobrazov adjusted Argan's settings to ensure that the Igroks could be used one after another in case a third shot proved necessary. He confidently configured the launch sequence created by Argan into his magic-calculation region. This time, he was determined to eliminate Tatsuya once and for all.

◇ ◇ ◇

Confirming Tuman Bomba's launch point, Tatsuya said to himself while reproducing Tuman Bomba's trajectory based on Trident's counterfire memory.

Target changed to the caster's CAD.

The relationship between a magician and his CAD became the most intimate during the process of casting magic. Information-wise, the CAD became a part of the magician, and the magician became a component of the CAD's magic system. This was true even when large CADs imposed magic on the magician. Tatsuya aimed at the Argan.

Objective: total destruction of the train car CAD.

Tatsuya could tell that a magic program had already begun taking form within the large CAD he saw in his mind's eye. At this point, it was still in the loading stage of the activation sequence. It seemed to be a complex activation sequence since loading was taking longer than a couple seconds.

Tatsuya's decomposition magic typically required the same amount of, if not greater, preparation. Luckily, his magic-calculation region specialized in decomposition and reconstruction magic. This meant the subsystems for these types of magic were preconfigured, allowing him to activate highly complex spells with the simple input of additional data. Therefore, he could execute complex processes, like breaking down matter to its elemental level and information bodies to their psionic level in a very short time.

Initializing Program Dispersion and Mist Dispersion.

In a matter of seconds, Tatsuya dispersed the interference force field surrounding Bezobrazov's large CAD, and Argan was disintegrated to its elemental form. Bezobrazov could consecutively activate two types of magic in an instant, despite the distance, thanks to the system he had prepared within his mind that sacrificed all other magic skills. Tatsuya activated one spell to disintegrate information bodies and another to collapse material forms at the very same time.

◇ ◇ ◇

At first, Bezobrazov thought there had been an earthquake. His vision seemed to blur, but his body didn't register any shaking. He suddenly felt as if he was falling, and this wasn't an illusion. The chair he was sitting on suddenly lost its ability to support his weight, and it wasn't just the chair. Argan's console, floor, and walls became completely unstable.

All of a sudden, the floor gave way, the ceiling collapsed, the walls crumbled, and everything seemed to turn to sand. Bezobrazov groaned as he was slammed hard against the ground. The pain was too intense to stand up immediately, and it wasn't just physical. His head throbbed severely from within. He couldn't think. The headache was so intense that he didn't even realize it came from the shock of his mind's forced disconnection from his Argan CAD.

He did, however, find the sand on his head annoying. Bezobrazov struggled to raise his upper body and brush the sand off his head. The realization that the sand was Argan's decomposed pieces was beyond his current mental capacity. It was only when he saw the scenery of Ussuriysk in front of him that he finally realized that he had been thrown outside.

Assailed by an intense headache, Bezobrazov sat down in a daze. The hearts of the three Igroks had stopped beating from the shock of being forcibly disconnected from the Argan CAD. Bezobrazov, however, was oblivious to the resulting commotion.

[9]

Though unsuccessful, the magical attack on First High was closely monitored. Among all the National Magic University-Affiliated High Schools, First High boasted the most advanced facilities. In terms of magic, the equipment for observing the school's campus rivaled even the National Defense Force's main bases.

First High's surveillance equipment provided objective data that a spell was cast atop the school to generate and explode hydrogen peroxide gas. The equipment also indicated that the spell originated from the New Soviet Union's coastal region.

The Magic University relayed this data to the government. As a result, the Minister of Foreign Affairs had enough evidence to strongly condemn the New Soviet Union for their act of aggression and to call for international sanctions against them.

The comments from the Minister of Industry, acting on behalf of Aoba Toudou, were even more critical. Though acknowledging that it was speculation, the minister announced that the failed attack could likely be traced back to Bezobrazov, the New Soviet Union's Thirteen Apostles member. Serious doubts began to be cast on the peaceful nature of the Dione Project, which Bezobrazov backed.

◇ ◇ ◇

It was Saturday, June 22. Tatsuya and Miyuki were watching the news of the previous day's press conference over breakfast.

"Well, this is lucky," Tatsuya mumbled.

"Is it? I thought you would have at least foreseen this much," Miyuki teased from across the table.

A wry smile appeared on Tatsuya's face as he shook his head. "Well, I didn't. My interception of Tuman Bomba at school was a complete coincidence. I actually thought the chances of an attack during the day were pretty small."

"So not even you can predict everything."

"Of course not."

Minami's hospitalization was one of the awful things that Tatsuya hadn't predicted. He pushed those regrets to the back of his mind so Miyuki wouldn't notice, and he forced a smile. The television screen transitioned to another newscast, and they continued their breakfast.

"In any case," said Miyuki, "I am sure this will dramatically shift the current public opinion."

Although the news had changed, her mindset had clearly not.

"That's true," said Tatsuya. "We can expect many more people to be against the Dione Project, at least in Japan."

He knew people were still speaking badly about him, but he had no intention of hiding from it. The Dione Project was born from conspiracies, after all. There was no need for him to feel guilty about using public opinion to crush a scheme that wanted to exile him to space.

"Either way, you will be continuing with the ESCAPES Plan, right?" Miyuki asked Tatsuya.

"Of course. The ESCAPES Plan was never meant to counter the Dione Project. My announcement's timing only pushed it in that direction. To tell the truth, I would have liked more time to prepare, but once I announced the plan, there was no turning back."

"I know. And I believe what you are doing is right."

She probably would have said the same thing if had Tatsuya sought world domination. But this was meaningless speculation. Tatsuya's goal was and had always been the peaceful use of magic.

"By the way," Miyuki added, "didn't Aunt Maya suggest you take a look at Miyaki Island?"

"Yeah, I've been thinking about that, too. It worked out too perfectly that she just let me have the island for the ESCAPES Plan when she was trying to turn it into a research facility."

"She must believe your plan will serve the Yotsuba family well."

"I hope you're right. Thanks for breakfast." Tatsuya laid down his chopsticks.

Though she was not finished eating yet, Miyuki sprang to her feet.

"I will go make you a cup of coffee," she said and scurried to the kitchen.

◇ ◇ ◇

The breakfast conversation at the Shiba household had naturally turned to a discussion of Miyaki Island. It wasn't that either of them had some kind of premonition. But when the topic was reopened by a visitor who stopped by before dinner, Tatsuya couldn't help remembering that morning's casual chat.

A girl stood in the doorway with an awkward smile.

"H-hi there...," she said, waving.

"Lina?!" Miyuki gasped.

Sure enough, their guest that evening was Angelina Kudou Shields.

"Sorry for coming by so late at night," Ayako said from Lina's side.

"That's not a problem. It's still before dinnertime," Tatsuya replied, staring at Lina with as much surprise as Miyuki. "Anyway, come on in."

"Yes," Miyuki quickly added, beckoning the two girls inside the apartment. "Please make yourselves at home."

"Thanks," Ayako told her. "Come on, Miss Shields."

"R-right… Thanks," Lina managed.

The two girls walked past Miyuki and followed Tatsuya into the living room; Ayako seemed right at home, while Lina looked reluctant.

"There was a mutiny, and you had to leave the country?" Tatsuya asked in surprise.

"How awful," Miyuki said.

After Ayako had explained the situation, Tatsuya and Miyuki were beside themselves with shock. Under normal circumstances, it would have been hard to believe, but they didn't see any reason for Lina to deceive them. They accepted the story as truth.

"The Kuroba family has been providing Miss Shields—I mean, Major Sirius—with temporary refuge, but Maya suggested she go into hiding on Miyaki Island," Ayako explained.

"Is there something Lina can do there?" Tatsuya asked her.

"The family seems to think so, but we're worried Major Sirius won't be satisfied with the environment."

"I'm not that picky," Lina mumbled.

"Anyhow," Ayako continued, ignoring Lina's comment, "we thought she should go ahead and take a look at the island."

"Has Aunt Maya already given her permission?" Miyuki asked, also paying Lina's comment little mind.

Lina shrank into herself, and although Tatsuya noticed this, he simply smiled uncomfortably and said nothing.

"She did." Ayako nodded. "She even suggested Tatsuya be the one to show the major around."

"Oh?" Miyuki seemed surprise.

"Interesting," Tatsuya said in a matter-of-fact tone. "It sounds like Aunt Maya thought, as a fellow strategic magician, I would be the most suitable person to restrain Lina in case her exile is a lie, and her true objective is to sabotage the Yotsuba family."

"But it's not!" Lina yelled, springing to her feet.

"I know." Tatsuya was finally paying attention to her. "Aunt Maya doesn't doubt you, either. She is only doing this to defend herself from possible criticism from the rest of the family."

"O-oh...," Lina stammered.

She had struggled through enough red tape in her career to understand what Tatsuya was talking about.

Tatsuya turned back to Ayako. "What are your plans for today?"

"I would love to stay over, but the clan head ordered me to give her your answer right away."

"So she doesn't trust phones, huh? Fine. Tell Mother that I accept the job."

"All right."

"It's too late to go to Miyaki Island today," Tatsuya continued. "We can go tomorrow. I'll be taking Miyuki with me, so tell Hanabishi to strengthen the security around Minami."

Interestingly, his orders were not for Hyougo but for his father.

"I will," Ayako said.

Tatsuya nodded and turned to Miyuki. "Could you prepare a room for Lina to stay the night?"

"Of course."

"H-hold on!" Lina protested.

Everything seemed to be happening without her consent, but the other three ignored her once again.

"My apologies for the abrupt visit. I will see you two later," Ayako said.

"Right. Let's find a time to sit down and talk soon," Tatsuya said.

"That would be great." Ayako grinned. "Fumiya and I would love that."

Miyuki walked Ayako to the door. "Thank you for bringing Lina to us today."

"You're welcome. Until next time."

Once Miyuki had closed the door and walked back to the living room, Tatsuya turned to Lina with a serious expression.

"I want to hear exactly what happened," he said to her.

"Me too," Miyuki added. "Have the parasites truly returned?"

Unable to escape Tatsuya and Miyuki's solemn request, Lina took a deep breath and began to explain.

(*To be continued in the Invasion Arc*)

Afterword

What did you think about the *Escape Arc*, published consecutively over two months in Volumes 24 and 25? Did you enjoy it?

Tatsuya escaped the Dione Project, thanks to his ESCAPES Plan, Minoru escaped his weak body, Raymond escaped his fate as a secondary character, and Lina escaped the USNA.

Clearly, there were many types of escapes in this two-part arc. I originally had a different subtitle in mind, but I knew it had to be the *Escape Arc* once I'd finished writing. Not to brag, but I think it's a very good title.

I thought of bringing Gongjin Zhou back when I was writing Volume 15 to help build Minoru up into a final-boss-type character. The scene in Volume 15, *Ancient City Insurrection Arc, Part 2*, where Tatsuya gazes upstream the Uji River serves as foreshadowing for the events in the *Escape Arc*.

Tatsuya can't see any spirits at the time, but the consequences of him brushing off an eerie feeling can be seen in Volume 24. In fact, you could say Tatsuya's actions in this scene lead directly to the creation of the formidable Minoru-Gongjin-Parasite adversary. Tatsuya doesn't necessarily feel responsible for this, though. He isn't the type of protagonist to feel guilty about things like that.

Minoru definitely made his way up as the last boss of the *Escape Arc*, but Minami made a big splash for herself in this arc as well. You could even say she became a heroine with the way Tatsuya and Minoru are fighting over her (LOL). This may seem like strange foreshadowing, but please look forward to seeing how everything pans out in future volumes.

As you may have noticed, Lina is finally making a full return to the main storyline. I had to introduce quite a few new characters to bring her back to Japan. I mean, Deneb didn't even have any lines. Shaula was also such a minor character that I hesitated to even mention her name. Anyway, this was how the two Stars members who debuted in the movie made an unexpected appearance in the novel's main storyline.

Bezobrazov's story reached a pseudo-conclusion in this volume, but he's not completely done just yet. Without giving too much away, I'll say he plays an important role in the return of Lirei Liu. Or you could say he has been given another chance to appear because my editorial team wants Lirei Liu back in the spotlight (LOL).

Recently, there have been fewer appearances of both First High students and alumni, but now that Tatsuya has returned to First High, they'll soon have opportunities to shine again. After adding so many more characters beyond my initial plan, I feel like there's much more to write about. But don't worry; to make up for the additional volumes, I will be increasing the pace of publication accordingly.

Anything I can't cover in the main storyline will probably be carried over into the *University Arc*. If I ever publish the *University Arc*, that is.

Anyway, putting uncertain elephants in the room aside, I'll be diving into the next volume of this series once I finish a spin-off for my official website. And who knows, I might even receive some work related to Bushiroad's *Triple Monsters*!

No matter what happens, I promise not to keep you waiting too long for Volume 26. I'm really hoping to speed up both the publishing pace and the story's plot development.

I look forward to seeing you all again in Volume 26, *Invasion Arc*. Thank you for reading.

Tsutomu Sato

HAVE YOU BEEN TURNED ON TO LIGHT NOVELS YET?

86—EIGHTY-SIX, VOL. 1–13

In truth, there is no such thing as a bloodless war. Beyond the fortified walls protecting the eighty-five Republic Sectors lies the "nonexistent" Eighty-Sixth Sector. The young men and women of this forsaken land are branded the Eighty-Six and, stripped of their humanity, pilot "unmanned" weapons into battle...

Manga adaptation available now!

WOLF & PARCHMENT, VOL. 1–10

The young man Col dreams of one day joining the holy clergy and departs on a journey from the bathhouse, Spice and Wolf. Winfiel Kingdom's prince has invited him to help correct the sins of the Church. But as his travels begin, Col discovers in his luggage a young girl with a wolf's ears and tail named Myuri, who stowed away for the ride!

Manga adaptation available now!

SOLO LEVELING, VOL. 1–8

E-rank hunter Jinwoo Sung has no money, no talent, and no prospects to speak of—and apparently, no luck, either! When he enters a hidden double dungeon one fateful day, he's abandoned by his party and left to die at the hands of some of the most horrific monsters he's ever encountered.

Comic adaptation available now!

THE SAGA OF TANYA THE EVIL, VOL. 1–13

Reborn as a destitute orphaned girl with nothing to her name but memories of a previous life, Tanya will do whatever it takes to survive, even if it means living life behind the barrel of a gun!

Manga adaptation available now!

SO I'M A SPIDER, SO WHAT?, VOL. 1–16

I used to be a normal high school girl, but in the blink of an eye, I woke up in a place I've never seen before and—and I was reborn as a spider?!

Manga adaptation available now!

OVERLORD, VOL. 1–16

When Momonga logs in one last time just to be there when the servers go dark, something happens—and suddenly, fantasy is reality. A rogues' gallery of fanatically devoted NPCs is ready to obey his every order, but the world Momonga now inhabits is not the one he remembers.

Manga adaptation available now!

VISIT YENPRESS.COM TO CHECK OUT ALL OUR TITLES AND. . .

GET YOUR YEN ON!

YEN ON

Yen Press